Dog Star

Dog Star

MEGAN
SHEPHERD

FARRAR STRAUS GIROUX
NEW YORK

Farrar Straus Giroux Books for Young Readers
An imprint of Macmillan Publishing Group, LLC
120 Broadway, New York, NY 10271
mackids.com

Our books may be purchased in bulk for promotional, educational, or
business use. Please contact your local bookseller or the Macmillan
Corporate and Premium Sales Department at (800) 221-7945 ext. 5442 or
by email at MacmillanSpecialMarkets@macmillan.com.

Library of Congress Cataloging-in-Publication Data
Names: Shepherd, Megan, author.
Title: Dog star / Megan Shepherd.
Description: First edition. | New York: Farrar Straus Giroux, 2021. |
Audience: Ages 8–12. | Audience: Grades 4–6. | Summary: Nina, a young
girl unsure of her role in her communist society, befriends a dog named
Laika, who dreams of finding a home and is being studied in Nina's father's
lab as part of the Soviet space program
Identifiers: LCCN 2020047134 | ISBN 9780374314583 (hardcover)
Subjects: LCSH: Laika (Dog)—Juvenile fiction. | Soviet Union—
History—1953–1985—Juvenile fiction. | CYAC: Laika (Dog)—Fiction.
| Soviet Union—History—1953–1985—Fiction. | Friendship—Fiction. |
Communism—Fiction.
Classification: LCC PZ7.S54374 Do 2021 | DDC [Fic]—dc23
LC record available at https://lccn.loc.gov/2020047134

First edition, 2021
Book design by Aurora Parlagreco
Printed in the United States of America by LSC Communications,
Harrisonburg, Virginia

ISBN 978-0-374-31458-3 (hardcover)
1 3 5 7 9 10 8 6 4 2

For my little beastie, R.

We were born to make fairy tales come true.
　—a line from the Soviet Air Force official march, 1936

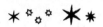

Dog Star

1

NAMELESS

IT WAS NO KIND OF night for a dog to be alone. A blast of wind howled down the streets of Moscow, firing pellets of snow against buildings. Not a person was out. No cars passed by. Every person who could was closed up in their home, enjoying a warm supper and the company of family. Outside, under the overhang of a shoe-store stoop, a little dog curled against the storm.

The dog was nameless. Only Warm Dogs were given names: dogs who lived in houses and ate from bowls and snuggled with children beneath warm blankets. Cold Dogs—the ones on the streets—had no use for names. The little dog thought only of her next meal. The mouse she'd caught two days ago no longer filled her belly. This was the Winter of Many Snows, when food was scarce. She'd survived two winters before, but this could be her last.

From the darkness came a snarl.

The little dog sprang to her feet. Snow stung her eyes as she squinted into the wind. Streetlamps outside the shoe store flickered weakly, revealing nothing.

The snarl came again.

Three Cold Dogs stalked into the light. She had crossed paths with two of them before. The grizzled old black one with the missing eye and the brindle who towered three times her height. The third dog was still a pup—it must have been his first winter—and desperation shone in his eyes.

This was not the first time the little dog had to defend her territory. It had taken weeks of scouring the city to find a place tucked away from the street, protected from the wind. A family of mice lived in the walls, drawn to the smell of the cobbler's kitchen. Most important, the steps blocked the view from the road where the dogcatcher stalked the streets.

The little dog bared her teeth against the intruders.

"*Back!*" she snarled.

The old black dog lowered his head and growled a low warning. "Run away, little one. We're taking this stoop."

The little dog stood her ground. "Get back!"

The pup began pacing. Judging by the lack of scars on his snout, he hadn't been in many fights and was anxious to prove himself.

The black dog gave a meaningful look to the brindle, who slunk forward into the light.

"This stoop belongs to us now," the brindle threatened.

"It's mine!" the little dog growled.

The brindle looked back at the one-eyed dog.

"You are alone," the old dog said in a gravelly bark. "You have no pack. You have no mate or pups. Dogs do not survive alone."

The little dog lifted her head, her eyes unwavering. "The *only* way to survive is to be alone."

The cold ground was freezing on the pads of her paws. Despite her raised hackles, she was shivering.

The pup started pacing again. The two older dogs exchanged a look, and then the black dog nodded. The brindle bared his teeth.

"It isn't your choice."

The brindle lunged. His claws tore through the fresh-fallen snow. The little dog braced herself. As he swiped at her, she twisted nimbly away and sank her teeth into his shoulder. Then the pup lunged with an oversize snarl. His teeth sliced at her as she shielded her eyes. A sting of pain ripped through her front paw. The pup snapped again, taking a chunk of fur from her ear.

The old black dog watched, his one yellow eye unmoving.

The brindle lunged for her again, and she dove into a broken crate just big enough for a pair of shoes—just big enough for a little dog. When she pressed herself against the far end, not even the lanky pup's scrambling claws could reach.

"Back!" the little dog ordered from the safety of her crate. "This stoop is mine!"

The pup kept snarling at the open end of the crate. The brindle sniffed around the outside, searching for weak boards. Inside, the little dog breathed fast. She ignored the sting of pain. If she lost the safety of her territory, she wouldn't survive another day.

At last, the black dog stood. With a grunt to the brindle and the pup, he turned and disappeared back into the storm. The pup whined, but after a sharp bark from the brindle, he retreated as well.

The little dog's breathing was ragged. She shivered from tail to snout. Pain throbbed in the bites on her paws and head. She waited as long as she dared and then crept out of the crate. There was no sign of the pack. She licked the wounds on her front paw.

It wasn't a question of whether the pack would return, only when.

For a brief moment, the storm lightened, and the little dog felt a break from the bitter cold. Soft rays of light shone down on her. From behind the broken clouds, the stars were coming out.

The little dog blinked up at the brightest one, the Dog Star.

"Thank you," she barked softly.

The star shone in glowing pulses. The little dog felt a gentle voice deep within her heart—the voice of the Dog Star.

You saved yourself, little one. You were brave. Soon there will come a time when you will need to be brave again.

All dogs—Cold Dogs and Warm Dogs and even the Wild Dogs who dwelt in the forest and spoke in howls—honored the Dog Star. Though his ways were mysterious, the Dog Star ruled the fates of all dogs, watching over them, guiding them, loving them from his celestial seat in the night sky.

As the little dog curled up in her crate, her eyelids began to fall. Every muscle ached. Surrendering to sleep, she heard the Dog Star add softly:

Braver than any dog has ever been.

2

NINA

THE MOMENT THAT NINA STEPPED inside the midnight-blue circus tent, her lips fell open in wonder. Thousands of candles hung from gossamer ropes to look like a sky full of stars. Outside, it was a gray, blusteringly cold night, but within the tent, giant torches threw out rippling waves of heat. It was as though she had stepped into a magical new world.

Still, despite the warmth, she tightened her scarf around her neck.

"Nina, keep an eye on your brother." Mama was frowning in Ivan's direction. He was already disappearing into the crowd, pushing his way toward the popcorn cart. He had turned ten the week before and seemed to have decided that he was now an adult, capable of setting his own bedtime and reading Papa's newspapers over breakfast.

Mama continued, "Your father needs undisturbed time with his colleagues from the Institute. Remember, we are here for his research, not your amusement. I expect you to keep your brother out of trouble." Her eyes settled on the knotted tassels of Nina's scarf and then went wide with recognition. "Take that scarf off." She paused. "It's warm in here. You don't need it."

Nina dug her fingers into the soft folds of the scarf. Though it was made of sturdy, warm wool, it felt like silk against her fingers. The first time she'd seen it, around the neck of her best friend, she'd thought it was the most beautiful thing in the world. It was sky blue—a color rarely seen in Moscow winters—with delicately embroidered pink and orange flowers and thick oversize tassels that tickled her chin.

"But it belonged to Ludmilla," she argued.

"*Shhh!*" Lowering her voice, Mama explained, "That's exactly the problem. Everyone remembers a scarf like that. And we don't want people recalling our connection with Ludmilla or any of the Sokolov family. What if Director Sonin sees you wearing it?" Mama's eyes slid to one of the men standing with Papa, the one with glasses and a scalp so bald it shone in the torchlight.

Nina clenched her jaw to keep from saying something she'd regret. Ludmilla had been her best friend since even before they were born—their mothers had been pregnant at the same time. They'd gone from throwing tea parties for their dolls to sneaking off together during school ceremonies, hiding behind Soviet banners to flip through contraband American magazines and try on lipstick borrowed from their mothers' purses. But Ludmilla, along with her family, had disappeared a week ago. The day before Ludmilla vanished, she'd pulled off the scarf and thrust it into Nina's hands. *I know you've always liked it*, she'd said. *Take it. Wear it so you don't forget me.*

At the time, Nina had only laughed. *You're just going on holiday, not to the moon.*

But Ludmilla had never returned to class.

Now every time Nina wound the woolen fabric around her neck, it felt like Ludmilla was still with her. Sky blue. The color of Ludmilla's eyes.

She unwound the scarf and shoved it into her coat pocket.

Mama's expression softened. "Here. Popcorn will warm your spirits." She pressed a coin into Nina's hand before joining Papa back at the tent entrance. Nina looked down at the coin in her palm and sighed. As though popcorn could take the place of a best friend.

Nina searched through the crowd for Ivan and found him pressed into a group of children clustered around a fortune-teller's table. An old woman with glittering gold earrings loomed over animal skulls and crystal balls.

"Tell me, children," the woman said, holding up a deck of cards covered with illustrations of crowns, skulls, and daggers. "Who among you is brave enough to have your fortune read?"

The other children shrieked and backed away, but Nina's ears perked up. "I'll do it."

Ivan tugged on her arm. "Nina, don't! My teacher says superstition is dangerously backward. She says it's as bad as religion."

Nina rolled her eyes. "And who will tell, eh? I seem to remember a boy who, just last summer, used to tie extra trousers around his waist and chase me through the house, claiming to be the six-legged Bukavac." She poked him teasingly in the side. She'd expected Ivan to smile at the memory, but instead he frowned harder.

She turned to the fortune-teller. "I want to know what will happen in the future." She twisted her fingers into the scarf in her pocket. "If things can ever go back to the way they were."

Ivan drew in a sharp breath. "I'm going to tell Papa!"

"Wait!" Nina called after him as he scurried into the crowd. But the tent was thick with people, all of them breathing heavily, the sound of crunching popcorn and crumpled tickets beneath their boots. Finally she caught sight of Ivan's gray felt hat bobbing between the tiger cage and the main stage.

She pushed toward the stage, where a mustachioed performer in a red hat was feeding beans to a monkey perched on his shoulder. The monkey had small black eyes and a pink face surrounded by golden fur. When the man held out his arm, the monkey ran down it and onto a stool. The crowd cheered as he bowed and took his monkey backstage.

She caught up to Ivan just as he reached Papa, who was wearing his brown military jacket with the red epaulets on the shoulders and had been deep in a hushed conversation with his colleagues. Now the conversation stopped. Papa looked sternly at Ivan behind his thick brown beard, then at Nina. So did the others, including Director Sonin. Nina drew in a sharp breath. These men and women were the scientists who did top secret work on rocket ships and outer space. Scientists who kept Papa at the Institute of Space Medicine, an hour's drive from Moscow, so late that sometimes she'd hear him come in after midnight and leave again before breakfast. Scientists who had been irate when Ludmilla's father had been granted rare permission to have his family accompany him to his astronomy conference in America, only to never return.

"What is it, Ivan?" Papa asked, but his eyes went to Nina, who at two years older than her brother was usually the wiser one. "Nina?"

Nina grabbed Ivan's hand hard and quickly said, "We were . . . wondering if we might watch you work on the Starflyer mission. We won't say a word." When her comment was met with cold silence, she added, "For the glory of the Motherland."

Papa's face broke into a smile. "Ah, you hear that, comrades? My daughter, such a good Communist."

"She makes the future of the Soviet Union look bright," one of the female scientists added with a smile.

But Papa's boss wasn't smiling. Director Sonin's eyes

drifted to the sky-blue scarf that had slipped out of Nina's coat pocket in her hurry and was now dangling toward the floor. Quickly, Nina stuffed it back into her pocket and hoped he hadn't recognized it as having belonged to a traitor.

"What do you know about the Starflyer mission, Nina Konstantinova?" Director Sonin asked in a low voice.

Warmth crept up her neck. Suddenly she wondered if she'd said too much. Though the details of the Institute of Space Medicine's work were top secret, the government-run radio and newspapers had been hinting of a bold new space mission that would put their American rivals to shame. Every newspaper carried speculation: Who would be the first to conquer space, America or the Soviet Union?

She stammered, "Ah . . . it's a program to train animals to ride in rocket ships to see if people could ever live in space. And . . . it will doubtless ensure the Soviet Union's supremacy not only on Earth but in the stars as well."

Director Sonin raised an eyebrow, glancing at her father. "I see. And can we trust you to keep what you see backstage today secret?"

She glanced at her father, who was watching her carefully. "Of course, sir."

Director Sonin nodded. "Then come with us. You too, my boy." He patted Ivan on the shoulder. "Meet the future heroes of the Starflyer mission: monkeys!"

Nina and Ivan exchanged a surprised look. *Monkeys?* In rocket ships? It was too wild to believe!

As she followed the scientists through the crowd, the loudspeaker announced that a constellation show was about to begin. The torchlights lowered, and the voice on the loudspeaker began to talk about times long ago, before lights and cities, when the stars lit the world and people found shapes in their positions. Papa held open a curtain to a backstage area, where several more scientists were speaking to the monkey trainer from the stage. The circus monkeys were in cages now. They didn't jump and swing and eat beans like in the show. They hunched over and scratched at bald patches on their backs.

". . . not suited for outer-space conditions," the trainer was saying. He had taken off both his red hat and, shockingly, his mustache. "Monkeys are sensitive to loud noises and extreme temperature changes. They might return to Earth wounded or with substantial trauma."

"Nevertheless," one of Papa's colleagues said, "we have trustworthy reports that American scientists intend to send apes into space and study the effects on them when they return. Their physiology makes them most similar to our human cosmonauts. If apes can survive the conditions, then it is likely that humans can, too."

"The Americans." Director Sonin gave a snort. "The Americans *are* apes. Isn't that right, little Communist?" He turned to Nina. She froze in place, unsure how to answer. She'd heard Mama and Papa whispering that Ludmilla's father was working for the Americans now—for the enemy—in a city called Boston, but anytime she brought it up, Mama and Papa hushed her immediately and darted to the window to see if any parked cars outside were watching.

"The Americans are indeed apes, sir," Nina replied.

He nodded, pleased. But the truth was, Nina didn't understand exactly *why* America was the enemy. If America was so awful, why had Ludmilla's family defected there? America had its charms, of course—the movie stars, the beautiful clothes, the vast mountains and forests—but everyone knew the Soviet Union was the greater nation. In America, women were expected to be only mothers and wives, whereas in the Soviet Union, they could serve as leaders and scientists, equals to men. In America, the poor lived on the streets, begging for scraps, whereas the Communist Party cared for each of its citizens and gave opportunities to all.

So why had the Sokolovs defected? Sergei Sokolov was a successful scientist and Ana Sokolov was the director of a good primary school. They'd shared their dinner table with Nina dozens of times. Why give up a good Communist life for America?

Nina glanced at her father, wishing she could ask him such questions. But she knew without being told that a good Communist didn't ask questions.

"We need an animal suited to harsh conditions," a female scientist said to Director Sonin. "An animal who has learned to adapt to unpredictable situations. To the cold, to small spaces. A clever animal, but one who will follow orders."

"But where to find such a one?" another scientist mused.

They were all quiet. Then Papa said, "I believe I know of one such animal."

Before Nina heard the rest of the conversation, her mother appeared at the backstage curtain, calling for them to come watch the constellation show. Nina and Ivan ran back through the curtain, beneath the candles moving overhead, forming glowing shapes of magical things, of moons and planets and constellations that kept watch over every part of the world, even as far away as Boston.

3

NAMELESS

THE STORM RAGED ALL NIGHT, until at last the hazy morning sun broke through the clouds. The little dog climbed out of her box. She inspected her wounds, licked them clean, then stretched out the tight muscles of her legs and back.

Her stomach whined with hunger.

She trotted over to the bin where the cobbler's family left their trash. She nosed through crumpled newspaper, scraps of wood, and nails, hoping for some small morsel of the family's breakfast. The faint aroma of cooking grease caught her nose, and she anxiously dug into the paper.

The shoe-store door swung open.

The little dog went as still as the concrete beneath her feet, the only movement that of her pounding heart.

The cobbler's wife stood with a sack of rubbish in one

hand, the other holding her robe closed. When her eyes fell on the dog, they flared.

"Scram!"

The little dog scrambled backward out of the rubbish bin, scattering newspaper everywhere. The wife yelled again. The dog charged down the alley. This was a game they'd played before, and she knew what was coming. Sure enough, a tattered old shoe grazed her rump as she raced toward the main street.

The wife yelled after her as she ran across the street and into the park with the high fence. She slowed to a trot, catching her breath. *Safe.* Soon the altercation was out of her mind, as her stomach growled again. There was another trash bin in the alley near the park, but as usual, the mice had already picked it clean. She set out on her usual course, checking the sewer grates and the bushes that sometimes held birds' nests. Outside the train station she found a paper wrapper with a crust of bread. She snatched it up before the other dogs who hung around the train station saw, and carried it two streets away to a patch of sidewalk in the sun, where she devoured the meager bites greedily.

She briefly closed her eyes, relishing the feeling of something—even something small—in her belly. When she opened her eyes, she found herself looking into the window of the house across the street. A little girl picked up a fat white dog and held it like a baby, rocking it back and forth. The dog didn't bite or scratch. It gazed up at the girl with big eyes.

Across the street, the little dog shivered. The sun had sunk behind a cloud. It would likely snow again during the coming night—she needed to scavenge for more food. But she couldn't take her eyes off the fat little dog. *A Warm Dog*, she thought. No shoes thrown at you. No licking old newspapers. No dog packs stalking your territory. Just kind children and warm blankets.

She turned away and caught her own reflection in the window behind her. Her ear was torn. Her back was dirty. She was bone-thin. How could the life of a Warm Dog ever belong to a street mutt like her?

She finished her circuit through the city, back to the shoe store, wary that the cobbler's wife might still be watching, but it was quiet. She nosed through the fresh trash—nothing. Her stomach demanded food. Reluctantly, she trotted over to the old shoe the wife had thrown. Shoe leather was a tough meal, but it wasn't the first time she'd been desperate enough to eat it.

She didn't see the two hands reach out of the shadows.

She jerked up with a snarl, but it was too late. The hands thrust a heavy cloth over her.

The dogcatcher!

She clawed frantically. The scent of people overwhelmed the air. Why hadn't she smelled their approach? She'd been thinking of that Warm Dog with his fat belly! How foolish! There were two of them, the people who had caught her: a woman in a hat that smelled like rabbit fur and a man who stank of tobacco.

The little dog scrambled hard enough to free her head from the cloth. She twisted and snarled but couldn't manage to bite the woman through the thick gloves she wore.

"*Shhh*," the woman urged.

The dog bared her teeth. Her heart fluttered as fast as the wings of a bird caught in a cat's mouth. Their truck reeked of rubber and was colored gray; not the dogcatcher's small white truck. If they weren't dogcatchers, who were they?

The woman drew a morsel from her pocket and the little dog stopped squirming. *Meat.* It smelled of delicious fatty juices. The woman set the meat on the ground. Then she set the dog down, too, and released her.

Time to run! the little dog thought. Her haunches were coiled to spring away. But her stomach whined, stopping her.

The meat smelled too good to leave behind.

The woman moved backward to give the dog space. Warily, the dog stepped forward. Raised her hackles and growled at the two people, who took another step backward.

She devoured the treat in a few anxious bites.

The taste of warm, juicy meat coated every inch of her tongue, awakening long-forgotten sensations in her mouth and stomach. She looked up at the woman, ready to bolt if needed. But the woman set down another treat. Then another. Each one was a little closer to the truck.

The dog growled another warning, and the man and

woman stepped back far enough that the dog knew she could outrun them if she needed to. She nibbled a treat that took her close to the truck's big tire. The next led her near the growling engine. The next took her through a tunnel of bent wires . . . where there sat an entire fat, greasy sausage!

She gulped and chewed and filled her yawning belly with the sausage. She didn't realize, until the man climbed high on the truck and reached behind her to close a door, that the bent wires she had entered were those of a cage.

The truck suddenly roared to life. *Caged!* The little dog's heart thunked as fast as the truck's engine. *Trapped!* She paced wildly. One step. *Turn.* Two steps. *Turn.* When she stood on her hind legs, she could just barely see out the truck's rear window.

The man was now behind the wheel. Where were they taking her? She scratched frantically at the wire bars as they passed buildings she didn't know. Streets and people and cars. She turned in panic, looking through the window on the opposite side. They were far from the shoe store now, and the growing distance pulled at her like a pup mewing for its mother. She whined. Gray buildings gave way to gray skies, which gave way to open fields dotted with trees.

After some time, the truck pulled up to a gate where men in stiff brown clothes exchanged muffled words with the driver. Soldiers opened the gate and the driver stopped the truck and got out. He came around and took out the dog's cage, wearing thick gloves so she couldn't bite him. She crouched in the corner, trembling. What was this place? A building the size of a city block, with arches and a domed roof and one, two, three, four . . . more windows than she could count. There were no displays of polished boots in the windows—not a shoe store. Many of the windows were boarded up with wood. She'd heard rumors of the *pound*—a terrible place where the dogcatcher starved his captives in freezing cold cages. But she didn't hear any barking or howls or sad baying, so maybe it wasn't a pound.

She watched and listened, awaiting her chance to bolt.

The driver carried her cage through a door flanked by soldiers. At once, the world grew darker. She cringed. She'd never been inside a building. There was no sky here, no gray clouds, no sun. She panted, needing air. Her eyes darted to one thing, then another. She had only hazy words for the people's odd-shaped constructions of wood and cloth and metal. *Chair? Curtains?*

But the scents . . . she knew those.

The smells were the same ones people carried when leaving their homes. Smells that older dogs had taught her were called *coffee* and *tobacco* and *boiled fish*.

The driver took her down a long hallway and she rose on all fours and sniffed. Another dog had been here. More than one. The sudden scents of dogs were almost too many: one musky, one faint, one that reeked of an old wound.

Was this the pound after all?

The driver set the cage on a table and the woman

in the rabbit-fur hat opened the latch. Other men and women wearing white coats watched with their heads cocked at an angle. One woman made scribbling marks on a piece of paper. The thick cloth was once more thrown over her. The little dog snarled, but something sharp stung her haunch. *A bee?* Now, in winter? Her paws began to feel heavy. Drool spilled out from the side of her mouth. When the woman lifted her from the wire cage, she found that she couldn't fight back.

The woman laid her on a metal table as slick as ice. Her eyes rolled partway back. Were those other dogs, there in the corner? In cages like hers? Or was she dreaming?

The people in white coats held pieces of long tape to her height, her length, and her width. They spoke in low voices. The little dog's eyelids lowered halfway. The view beyond the room's window grew hazy. The city felt very far away. When she escaped—and she must—how would she find her alley again?

The woman, who had removed her hat to reveal curls the color of sunlight, stroked the little dog with soft hands, murmuring words that the dog didn't understand.

"Laika. Laika."

They jabbed her again with that sharp sting like a bee, and her body went soft, her eyes sank all the way closed, and her heart jogged in fast little patters.

Sleep overtook her.

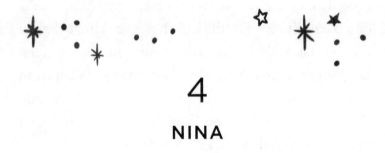

4

NINA

NINA'S SCHOOL WAS A DRAB gray building across the street from a park filled with drab gray statues. Mama walked her and Ivan the four blocks from their town house to the school, distractedly digging in her purse. Like most of the students headed into the school, Nina and Ivan wore the white shirt and red kerchief of the Young Pioneers, the youth organization that would prepare them to be good Soviet citizens through sports, service projects, and scouting games. As a sixth year, Nina had already been a Pioneer for three years and didn't mind it too much, except for the very loud anthems and very boring speeches. But Ivan, in year four, had joined the month before and had excitedly talked about little else since.

"Ivan, wait a moment," Mama ordered before he went inside. She straightened his Young Pioneer kerchief and fastened it with a gold pin she'd taken out of her purse.

She brushed off his shoulders. "There. You must make your father proud today at the Pioneers rally. I will hear from your teachers how well you sing 'Our Land.'"

"I'll make him proud, Mama."

She squeezed his shoulder. "You always do."

Nina rolled her eyes.

Mama checked her wristwatch and gasped. "The bell will ring soon! Remember, I will pick you up promptly after school for the meeting. Don't be late." She gave them a stern look. The Chief Designer, head over all of Papa's department, was holding a meeting at the Institute of Space Medicine about the Starflyer program and had requested that the scientists' families attend. Nina had never been allowed to visit her father's office before. It was in the countryside beyond the city, beyond the forests. She couldn't help but wonder if the meeting had something to do with the Sokolovs' defection.

Mama touched Nina's cheek. "You have your essay?"

"Yes, Mama."

Mama ran a finger down to the sky-blue scarf Nina had tucked into her coat. "Take this off as soon as you get to class, yes? You shouldn't wear it in public."

Nina looked away. "I will."

Mama placed a kiss on Ivan's head, checked her watch again, and hurried back down the street.

Nina made it to class just as the bell rang. She slid into her desk in the second-to-last row. Behind her, Tatyanna was bent over her own essay, pencil in hand, scratching

25

out a few words. They had been instructed to write about the person they knew who contributed the most to the Communist Party.

"Didn't you finish your essay?" Nina asked.

"Barely," Tatyanna confessed. "I was up half the night worried about it. I wrote about my uncle, a farmer in Kolomna. Now I'm afraid that farming isn't an honorable enough contribution to the Soviet Union workforce."

Nina unwound her scarf and stuffed it into the open drawer beneath her desk. If she closed her eyes, she could still picture Ludmilla wrapping it over her hair and putting on oversize sunglasses, pretending to be a movie star.

Tatyanna was staring at her.

Nina leaned close and said in a low-pitched imitation of their teacher, "All contributions are equal in the eyes of the Soviet Union." Their teacher, Olenka Ivanovna, had made each of them recite the phrase the week before until it had been fixed in their heads.

Tatyanna laughed but didn't look entirely convinced.

Olenka Ivanovna entered and stood before the blackboard. The students straightened in their seats.

"Grigory," the teacher announced, "you shall read first."

Grigory, in the first chair in the front row, stood nervously in front of the class, shifting from one foot to the other, as he read about his mother's work in the transportation department. One by one, the other students spoke about the person they knew who best contributed to the Communist Party. Nina felt her attention slide to the window.

She thought about the monkeys in their cages. The beautiful starry tent ceiling. Ludmilla would have loved the circus. Were there monkeys in Boston?

"Nina?"

She jerked to attention only to realize that the entire class was staring at her. The teacher must have called on her several times. Red flushed into her cheeks.

She grabbed her paper and hurried to the front of the classroom. She cleared her throat and began to read.

"The person I know who contributes the most to the Soviet Union is Konstantin Azarov, my father. He is a scientist at the Institute of Space Medicine. He and the men and women in his laboratory are working to move the Soviet Union from its agricultural past toward a great technological future. In his laboratory, he develops missiles, satellites, and . . ."

The other students started snickering, and Nina glanced up in confusion to see that Pyotr, who sat at the desk to her left, had reached into her desk drawer and taken out Ludmilla's scarf. He was pretending to wipe his underarms with it.

Shocked, Nina didn't know what to do. Their teacher hadn't seemed to notice, and instead was watching Nina with an impatient look.

Nina cleared her throat and continued, ". . . and rockets that will lead the Soviet Union to become the first nation to send a person into space, when our Motherland will forever be known as an advanced world power."

She stole a glance back at Pyotr. He was still wiping the scarf under his arms, contaminating it with his stink. She felt her hands begin to shake with anger.

She continued tightly, "Sending a human into space requires my father to work long hours. He and his comrades develop . . . develop test launches with nonhuman passengers. They have sent radio equipment into space, and soon they may even send an animal. They call these valiant creatures 'animal cosmonauts' on the radio news programs. Without scientists like my father, the Americans would . . . would . . ."

She could hear the children snickering louder. She focused on the paper, telling herself to ignore Pyotr. "The Americans would . . ." Her face burned. Her hands were shaking so badly that she couldn't read her own writing. ". . . Eat us?"

The class burst out in laughter.

Nina felt her heart stop. "No, no. *Beat* us. The Americans would beat us in the race to put a man in orbit . . ." Her words were drowned out by laughter. Furious, she crumpled the essay in her fist and threw the tight paper ball at Pyotr with all her strength. "You're just mad because Ludmilla wouldn't hold your hand behind the stadium at the spring rally!"

Pyotr's face went white.

Olenka Ivanovna rapped on her desk, calling for silence. "Take a seat, Nina," she said sharply. "That kind of outburst is uncalled for. I'd like to speak to you after school."

"But Pyotr started it."

"Enough!"

Nina stomped back to her desk. Her heart was pounding. She sat anxiously through the Young Pioneers rally at lunch, where Ivan sang "Our Land," and her afternoon classes, preparing her argument that everything was Pyotr's fault. But she was surprised when Olenka Ivanovna didn't want to talk about Pyotr.

"This isn't about him, is it?" Olenka Ivanovna said sternly.

"Of course it is." Nina blinked, confused. "Who else would it be about?"

Her teacher frowned deeper. "I saw the blue scarf in your desk, Nina. Everyone knows Ludmilla Sokolov was your closest friend. It must have been difficult to learn of their treachery."

Nina reluctantly muttered what her mother had told her to say. "We've denounced their family."

Olenka Ivanovna nodded, pleased with this. "Good. Pyotr was rightfully angry that we had a traitor in our midst. In our very classroom. You don't want to be seen as a friend to a traitor, do you?"

Nina shoved her hands into her pockets. She was angry but also filled with questions. How did living in a different city and speaking a different language make the Sokolovs the enemy? She glanced at the window. Mama would arrive soon to pick her up. "No."

Olenka Ivanovna leaned forward. "You must strive

to be more like your brother. At the assembly today Ivan brought a tear to my eye when he sang 'Our Land.' An exemplary young man. Perhaps if he were a bit older, he would have reported Ludmilla to the authorities himself."

Nina's chest tightened with anger. Ivan would never report on a friend.

"No one *reported* Ludmilla's family," she said. "The authorities discovered their defection on their own."

Olenka Ivanovna's eyebrows rose. "I don't know where you heard that, but you must have misunderstood." She leaned back in her chair proudly. "The Sokolov betrayal was discovered by our school's own students. Ludmilla was volunteering at the state orphanage as part of a Young Pioneers project, and some of the other Pioneers overheard her spreading lies about how the Soviet Union starves its people and sends dissenters to labor camps." She made a disgusted face. "Naturally, the students reported her to School Director Stepko, who reported her to the authorities. The Soviet government was prepared to detain Ludmilla's family when they returned from their trip to America, but of course, they never did return."

Nina felt her head spinning.

"The Young Pioneers reported her?" she asked, convinced she must have heard wrong. She'd always thought of the Young Pioneers as a group that taught them to tie knots and help old people across the street.

"It's a commendable organization," her teacher said proudly.

Nina felt like an icy wave had crashed into her, chilling her to the bone.

Outside the school, the wind was fierce, the sky threatening more snow. She opened her satchel and found Ludmilla's scarf. She wrapped it around her neck, tucking it deep into her coat collar so it wasn't visible.

"Nina!" a voice called. She hunched in her coat as the boys from her class surrounded her. "Tell us again how the Americans are going to eat us."

She turned away sharply.

Pyotr laughed again. Suddenly he shoved her arm, hard enough to bruise. He snaked his other hand into her collar and grabbed Ludmilla's scarf, pulling it off.

"Pyotr!" Nina swiped for it. "Give that back!"

"Why? It belonged to a traitor. You should have thrown it away the day Ludmilla defected." Pyotr held the scarf to his nose, grimacing. "Oof, this thing stinks of disloyalty! I would be doing you a favor by destroying it." He pulled his Young Pioneer pocketknife out of his coat and flicked open the blade.

Nina sucked in a breath. "Don't you dare. The only reason it stinks is because you rubbed it under your arms!"

She lunged for Pyotr, but he was faster. He danced backward, thrusting the sharp blade into the center of the beautiful fabric. With an awful twist of his hand, he sliced the scarf in two. Tassels fell to the ground. Threads snapped with a *pling*. He cut it apart again and again and again, dropping shredded pieces of wool at their feet. The rest of the scarf he stuffed into the trash can by the street.

As the other children shuffled away, Nina dug through the trash and managed to salvage a scrap of fabric with a tassel still attached. She cradled it in her hands.

The embroidered flowers were ripped, the threads tangled and torn. Her last token of Ludmilla—ruined.

A moment later, Mama's car pulled up.

When Nina slid into the back seat next to Ivan, still clutching the scrap of fabric, Mama turned around and looked at her face with wide eyes. "What happened?"

Nina wanted to tell her everything. She wanted to yell about Pyotr and ask questions, so many questions, but Mama had already told her many times to keep the scarf hidden, to forget she'd ever been friends with Ludmilla. So she shoved the scrap in her pocket and looked out the window, wiping the tears from her face.

"It's nothing."

Her mother met her gaze in the rearview mirror but didn't press. "We'll be at your father's office in half an hour. I expect you both to be on your best behavior."

Nina's mother was pulling at the skin around her throat, as she did when she was nervous. Ivan didn't seem to notice Mama's worry. He sat up excitedly. "Are we going to see the monkey cosmonauts?"

"I don't think so," Mama said distractedly. "Anyway, they decided not to use monkeys."

Ivan's face fell. "Then what will they send to space?"

Mama flipped on the radio. She cleared her throat. "Dogs, I think."

Nina looked at her mother in surprise. "Dogs? Dogs like people's pets? Like dogs in the streets?"

"Of course. What other dogs would I be talking about?"

Nina sat back and watched out the window as she considered this. Monkeys felt as extraordinary as space travel itself . . . but dogs were completely ordinary in every way, just as ordinary as *she* was. She hadn't thought something as common as a dog could go to space.

She squeezed the scrap of fabric in her pocket. The more she thought about it, the more she thought she'd like to see a dog fly to the stars. She'd like to believe that something amazing could happen to everyday creatures, whether it was a dog or just a girl.

5

LAIKA

WHEN THE LITTLE DOG WOKE, she was back in the wire cage. She sprang to her feet. Her haunches coiled out of instinct, ready to bolt. As her vision cleared, she studied the room. It was filled with a few people-objects she knew—a *chair* and a *fireplace*—and many she didn't. The people in white coats were gone, but there were two other dogs in cages. Her fur bristled as she remembered the street fight with the one-eyed old dog, the brindle, and the lanky pup whose wounds she still bore on her paws.

When one of the dogs—a fluffy cream-colored one with a black spot on her face—saw that the little dog was awake, she jumped to her feet, barking excitedly.

"Hey, you!"

The second dog, her age written in the wiry, thinning hairs clustered around her eyes and snout, only blinked sagely, as though she had met many dogs in many cages and it was nothing to bark about.

"Hey! Hey, you!"

The old dog snapped at the other. "Won't you be quiet? Keep barking like that and you'll wake the people and get a scolding." She turned to the little dog. "She's been like this day in, day out. She only got here a few days ago. There's no reasoning with her. I'm Albina, and this is . . ."

The other dog yipped again.

"Mushka," Albina finished for her with a sigh.

The little dog looked at them warily, but with the bars between them, she was safe—at least for now. There was no danger of them attacking her like the pack in the alley had. "You have names? Are you . . . Warm Dogs?"

"Oh stars!" Albina rolled her head in amusement. "Hardly. Well, this one was." She nodded toward the dog with the spot on her face. "Mushka climbed out an open window in her home and chased after a deliveryman. The people in white coats mistook her for a Cold Dog." She paused. "They only ever take Cold Dogs."

Mushka sat down and whined to herself. "I had bacon in my breakfast bowl every morning. *Bacon!*"

"No one forced you to climb out the window and run away," Albina chided. She turned back to the little dog. "The people in white coats named us when we arrived, just like they did with you."

The little dog narrowed her eyes. She remembered so

little; her head was still foggy. "They named me? What did they name me?"

"Laika!" Mushka yipped.

Albina nodded. "It means 'One Who Barks,' though you strike me as a quiet creature. Quieter than this one, I hope." She directed her snout at Mushka.

The little dog sat down, digesting this information. *Lai-ka?* The word felt both odd and familiar at the same time.

"Is this a pound?" Laika asked.

"No," Albina said, chuckling. "All of you new dogs from the streets think it's a pound. It's called Star City. It was once a big home for very important people. This room is called the parlor. They keep dogs here to do tricks. There are only the three of us now, but often there are more. Dogs come and go."

Laika raised her nose cautiously. She smelled the distant echo of more dogs. The hairs on the back of her spine rose when she thought of how dogs that disappeared off the streets never came back.

"I have to get out of here," she said.

Albina gave her a long, piteous look. "Dogs do not escape from Star City."

Laika ignored the warning. She paced back and forth in her cage and pawed at the metal latch.

"Stop that," the old dog chastised. "The people are not cruel. You must trust them."

"I don't." Laika bared her teeth. "And I don't trust other dogs, either!"

Albina didn't seem offended. If she was truly another dog from the streets, then she was used to the fear one stray dog felt for another. Instead, she lowered her voice and asked, "So you don't want to know how the people might make us Warm Dogs?"

Laika kept her distance from the old dog, even with the bars between them. People had tempted her with poisoned words before, and there was no reason why dogs might not, too. "What do you mean, they might make us Warm Dogs?" She looked around the room. "There aren't any blankets here. There aren't any small children."

Albina's eyes sparkled with the wisdom she'd accumulated in her many years. "It isn't as easy as that. Not just any dog can become a Warm Dog. Only special ones. That's why we are here: to prove ourselves worthy."

Mushka stopped pitying herself over lost bacon and blinked up at Albina. "How do we prove ourselves?"

"By being good and obedient. By not barking at every pin drop." Albina eyed Mushka pointedly. "And by mastering the three tricks."

Laika gave her a sidelong look. "What tricks?"

Albina yawned. "Oh, a tough dog like you doesn't care about tricks." She started circling, ready to go to sleep, and then plunked down and closed her eyes.

"Wait!" Laika barked.

Albina opened one eye. "So you've decided to trust us?"

Laika took a step backward. "I didn't say that."

Albina lifted her chin knowingly. "I remember what it was like on the streets. The frost in your bones, the hunger. The dog packs. I was like you when they first brought me here." Albina shook off her sleepiness and announced, "All dogs in Star City strive to master three tricks: the Shake-Shake Box, the Spinning Storm, and the Black Eternity. Few dogs, if any, complete all three."

"What happens if we do?" Mushka asked in a hushed breath.

"You have seen birds jump from branches and soar in the wind, yes? Seen them glide from one tree to another? Seen them swoop above lakes without falling in?"

Laika and Mushka nodded.

Albina raised her white-whiskered chin, her wise eyes glistening. "Our ultimate mission is to fly."

Mushka jumped up. "Impossible," she barked. "We aren't birds!"

Laika kept her eyes fastened on the old white dog. She felt an odd tingling at the words. It spread to the pads of her paws and the tip of her tail. *Flying.*

Albina looked toward the window, which showed the moon beyond, fat and bright. "It is not impossible. I've done it. Years ago, I mastered the three tricks, and the people in white coats prepared me for a mission. I've flown twice in the people's flying capsules. It is loud. It is scary. But I did it, and I have faith that they will soon make me a Warm Dog as a reward."

The story sounded too good to be true. "How can you believe such a thing?" Laika scoffed.

Albina's eyes gleamed. "Because it happened to a dog who used to live here. Tsygan completed several missions, and the Man with Prominent Ears gave her a home. For the rest of her life, Tsygan shall have a full belly and children to pet her and snuggle with in blankets. And, with luck, so shall I."

Mushka had calmed down. She rested her chin on the wire bars and watched Albina with wide eyes, hungry for more of the beautiful story.

Laika paced. Anxious thoughts chased one another through her mind. Albina's description didn't sound like any people she had known. Her early memories were hazy: a cozy nest of old flour sacks, warm milk from her mother, and the comforting press of siblings while she slept. But it had vanished far too soon. The gleam of the dogcatcher's truck. The cries from her brothers and sisters. Her mother's bark for her to run as fast as she could and never come back.

She thought of the shoe-store stoop. A home, but a miserable one. The hard ground sending cold into her fur as she slept. The cobbler's wife who threw shoes at her. Mice so frail they slid down her throat in one unsatisfying swallow. The pack of dogs who would be back for another fight.

Could there possibly be a child out there to feed her and keep her warm? Laika felt a sudden tug in her belly, even though she was still full from sausage. A hunger for something *more* than food.

She looked down at the scars on her paws and her fur bristled. No. Other dogs had only ever hurt her. There was no reason to trust Albina.

She curled up in her cage and studied every corner of the room for a means of escape.

6

NINA

AS HER MOTHER DROVE TOWARD the Institute of
Space Medicine, Nina watched heavy clouds roll in overhead through the car's rear window.

"Are we going to actually see inside the laboratory?"
Ivan asked.

Papa had described a place of cavernous old rooms and
glittering steel equipment, but it remained a mystery.

Mama was twisting the car radio knob anxiously.
Static gave way to voices and then turned back to static.
"I doubt they'll allow children running around valuable
equipment," she said offhandedly. "Your father's work is
very important."

Nina hesitated. "Why does the Chief Designer want
to see us?"

Mama settled on a radio station and gripped the

steering wheel tightly, ear cocked toward the speaker. For a moment, she didn't speak.

"Is it about Ludmilla's family?" Nina continued in a quieter voice.

Mama cleared her throat. "Just remember what I told you to say. We've denounced them."

Nina felt a sharp pang in her stomach as she remembered a few nights after the Sokolovs had defected to America. She'd heard her parents whispering, muffled by the gush of the running kitchen sink, that if the Sokolovs ever returned, they'd be arrested, maybe even shot as traitors. In her pocket, she squeezed the scrap of blue scarf.

"Papa won't disappoint the Communist Party like Comrade Sokolov did," Ivan said.

Mama gave him a smile in the rearview mirror that didn't quite reach her eyes. "Of course not, darling."

Outside, a deer ran across a nearby field. Nina rolled down the window and stuck out her head, breathing in fresh air. It helped keep the worry in her heart at bay. The wind wove its fingers through her curls, and she closed her eyes, drawing in a breath before she rolled the window back up. On the other side of the glass, the deer vanished into the woods. The sky was dark with clouds.

The radio stopped playing classical music and a voice began. In the rearview mirror, Mama chewed nervously on her bottom lip.

"From the United States of America to Australia, the whole world will soon be watching the night sky. Our brave Party is

planning to launch what will become the first satellite to orbit the Earth, even to send a living creature into space, beyond Earth's atmosphere, where no being has trod . . ."

"Hey, that's about Papa's work!" Ivan said.

Mama nodded. "The government is starting to speak about the mission publicly. There's a lot of pressure on your father. The whole world will be watching. If this mission fails . . ." Her next words died in her throat. "The Chief Designer has high expectations for your father's team. He and the other administrators do not tolerate mistakes."

The radio continued, "*. . . fears that the United States might retaliate with violence . . .*"

Violence?

Mama clicked off the radio quickly.

"Wait," Ivan said, leaning forward. "I want to hear the rest."

Nina thought fast and made her fingers into a many-legged monster, tickling his arm. Though it had been a long time since they'd played such games, he laughed and swatted at her hand and forgot about the mention of violence.

Mama pulled the car up to a tall gate flanked by soldiers. Outside, the clouds broke into a thin, cold sleet. She showed her identification to a soldier, who placed a call on his intercom, then unlatched the gate, directing Mama to follow the signs to the laboratory's back entrance. Nina pressed her face to the window in wonder, marveling at the laboratory.

"Papa never said he worked in a castle!" she said.

She'd expected it to be like the government offices in Moscow, boxy gray concrete structures that all looked the same. But this looked straight out of a fairy tale. The Institute of Space Medicine was a beautiful mansion with columns of polished marble and ornate towers rising to the sky, all of it surrounding a parklike courtyard she could glimpse through the wrought-iron gate.

A smile tugged at Mama's face. "Not a castle, lapochka. But close. A palace." She bit her lip. "Well, at least it used to be. The government repurposed it as part of the Communist regime. When they overthrew the monarchy, they had no need for these old churches and palaces, so they made them into government buildings."

Now that Nina looked closer, she noticed the cracks in the marble, broken and boarded-up windows. The structure must once have been a beautiful palace but had been left to crumble for decades. Now its archways were marred by barbed-wire fences, the courtyard filled with military tents and trucks in the mud.

A woman wearing glasses and a white coat over her dress opened a door. Nina recognized her as one of the female scientists she'd seen at the circus.

Mama twisted around in the driver's seat to give her children a sharp look. "Behave yourselves, children. And not a word about the Sokolovs." She gave Nina an especially long look. "I mean it. No trouble."

"I'm not trouble," Nina argued.

Freezing rain stung Nina's face as they darted across

the mud to the laboratory entrance. The scientist waved them in, locking the door behind them. Nina tilted her head up, taking in the strict signs on the walls.

Authorized Personnel Only.
The Communist Party Requires Your Loyalty.
Worker, Be on the Alert!

"What awful weather!" the scientist said. The woman had a mole on her left cheek, thick golden hair, and kind eyes. She extended her hand to Mama. "Svetlana Popovich, veterinary officer. Thank you for making the trip. You must be Lidia."

Mama gave a small nod.

The scientist shook hands with Ivan and then Nina. Nina had never met anyone with such silky-soft hands before, hands she would have expected on an actress, not a researcher.

Mama was pinching the skin on her throat anxiously. "The secretary I spoke with on the phone . . . she didn't say what this meeting was about . . ."

"The Chief Designer will explain. He is with your husband in that last room on the left. The children can stay with me until he is ready to speak with them. We've already met with the other families. You're the last one." She turned to Ivan and Nina. "Would you two like to see where your father works? There are several unclassified projects I can show you."

"Oh, yes!" Ivan said and started rattling on about his model rockets at home.

Nina forgot about her mother as they followed Svetlana Popovich through a set of double doors into a large room that had once been a kitchen. Two men in white coats were using pliers on a shiny silver ball the size of a washing machine.

"Wow!" Ivan ran over to watch.

Nina folded her arms across her chest, looking around curiously. "Where are the dogs?"

Svetlana smiled. "Would you like to meet them?"

Nina shrugged, but excitement was buzzing in her chest. She still couldn't believe that plain old dogs might soon float amid the stars. Svetlana led her into a room that looked like it had once been a living room of the palace. There was a fireplace between the windows and an overstuffed chair stacked with files, only now the room also had canvas tarps on the floor and wire cages lining one wall. There were three dogs in the cages. These dogs weren't like pet-store dogs Nina had seen, well-groomed puppies wagging their tails in shop windows. These dogs were small, and their features weren't those of huskies or terriers or any breed that Nina had seen in her encyclopedia. These looked like the strays she saw out the school window rooting through trash.

"Oh!" Nina said in surprise. "They're strays?"

Svetlana laughed. "You were expecting purebreds? Ah, but look closely at these dogs. Loyal, strong mutts in the tradition of the great Russian physiologist Ivan Pavlov.

Dogs from the street, who are used to harsh temperatures, who have learned to adapt to unpredictable conditions. It cannot be denied that there is a humble nobility in the common dog. I selected these three myself." Svetlana's eyes shone with pride. "We are training all three to be starflyers, but only one will be selected to launch in the rocket."

"Which one?"

"The tests will determine that."

"Isn't it dangerous? To go into space? I mean, dogs can't pilot a rocket, can they?"

Svetlana smiled. "Of course not. We pilot the rocket through remote radio control, but as to your first question, yes. Any mission that involves complex calculations holds a risk, especially one that has never been done before. We and the Americans have both sent animals into the atmosphere, but only a few hundred feet high, never before into outer space. Sputnik II will go higher than any rocket ever has! The dog inside will attain weightlessness. As that has never happened before, no one knows the effects it will have on a living creature. How will she eat? Can a dog swallow without gravity? Will solar radiation affect her? What if a meteorite hits the rocket?"

Nina's eyebrows shot up in alarm.

Svetlana cleared her throat. "Don't worry. Our space program has an excellent track record. Many dogs have been sent into the atmosphere and returned unharmed. Your father and I and all of us are working hard to ensure a successful outcome for the program and for the passenger."

Nina touched the cage where an old dog with white hairs on her face was sleeping.

"They are friendly," Svetlana offered. "We selected them in part for their mild nature. That last one, however, is new. Best to give her some space."

Another scientist stuck his head in, holding up a file and calling Svetlana over. She rested a hand on Nina's shoulder. "I'll be just over here, by the door." She stepped away.

Nina wiggled a finger between the bars of the first cage, but the old dog kept snoring. She moved to the next cage. The second dog was cream-colored with a black spot on her face. She had a lolling pink tongue and yapped excitedly at Nina. Her little nails clicked on the cage floor. Nina took a step back. This one reminded her of the overeager students at the Young Pioneer rallies—the ones who sang at the top of their lungs and saluted so hard she was afraid they'd bruise their own foreheads.

She moved to the third cage, where a white dog with chocolate and tan marks around her face was sitting alone in the far corner. Her dark brown eyes were wary. She didn't bark, nor did she come when Nina stuck a finger between the wires. But she didn't growl, either. A small chalkboard hanging on her crate read *Laika*.

Nina looked over her shoulder at Svetlana, who was still talking to the other scientist. Nina wrapped her fingers around the cage wires and leaned in.

"Hello, Laika." Nina smiled. "You look like trouble."

The dog continued to study her with those keen brown eyes.

"Where did you come from? Did you run away from a family? Did someone throw you out?" She leaned in closer, examining a small tear in the dog's ear. It looked like a bite mark. And there were more wounds on the dog's paws and back, some old and scarred, others only recently healing, and coated with a salve that the medical officer must have applied.

Nina's heart softened.

"You poor thing." She touched the bruise on her own arm where Pyotr had shoved her. She, too, knew what it was like to feel small.

Nina whispered conspiratorially, "Did you know that you might go into space?" She nodded solemnly. "The whole world is watching. From America to Australia. You could be famous. A flying dog. Can you believe it?"

The dog looked at her warily. Nina realized the dog was shivering. "You are cold, poor girl!" She looked around the room for a blanket but found none. She thought of the pet-store puppies who had full bowls of food and water, squeaking toys, and knotted ropes to play tug-of-war. Before she realized what she was doing, she thrust her hand into her pocket and grabbed what was left of Ludmilla's scarf. The scrap she'd rescued from the trash was too small to be of use to a person, but it was a good size for a small brown-and-white dog. On impulse, she stuffed it between the bars. Her heart was skipping off-kilter. What had she done? It was all she had left of Ludmilla. For a brief moment she considered reaching through the bars and taking the scarf back, but then she straightened her shoulders.

"That's for you, little troublemaker," she whispered.

After a moment of caution, a flicker of curiosity crossed the dog's eyes, and she cocked her head. She looked intently at the scarf, then at Nina. Nina got the sense that, like those dogs she'd seen in the street, this one had known very little kindness from humans.

She rested her hand on the bars. "It's okay. You don't have to come closer. That scarf has kept me warm on even the coldest days. It'll keep you warm, too."

Hesitantly, Laika stepped forward and slowly pressed her nose against the tattered blue scarf.

Nina's face broke into a grin, but then a commotion to her side interrupted her.

"Ivan. Nina."

Papa stood in the doorway with the other scientists. Mama was by his side. Her face had gone white. She didn't look at the dogs. She clutched her purse tightly. Another man stood with them, one who was tall and had gray hair and graying skin the same color of the palace stone outside. And like the palace, he looked like he'd survived countless battles. Silver medals decorated his uniform.

"Papa?" Ivan asked. "Is your meeting over?"

Papa gave a tight smile. "Yes. Children, I would like to introduce you to the venerable Chief Designer."

Ivan immediately came to stand next to Nina, near the

crates. He saluted as they'd been taught to do in Young Pioneers. "Chief Designer, sir!" Ivan said with intense seriousness.

Nina straightened, unsure what to do. Was she supposed to salute? Mama hadn't said anything about saluting.

But the Chief Designer only smiled. He stepped into the room and leaned down so he was eye level with the two of them. "Ivan, is it? And Nina? Your father tells me you are both exceptional young Communists. That you do well in school and have memorized all the Young Pioneer songs."

"Yes, sir!" Ivan said. Nina felt herself nodding beside him, though she usually just mumbled through the songs.

The Chief Designer smiled. "Excellent." His gaze shifted to Nina. "And you, Nina. I understand you were very close with the Sokolov girl. Has she tried to get in contact with you? Sent you any letters?"

Alarmed, Nina glanced at Papa and Mama, whose faces were both pinched. "Um, no, sir."

"And did she ever talk to you about her family's plans?"

Nina answered more quickly this time. "No, sir."

The Chief Designer leaned in close to her ear, lowering his voice so that Ivan wouldn't hear. "She told you nothing about her father's work with our missile system? How much the Americans would pay for that information?"

Nina felt her eyes going big, but she fought to keep a straight face. Missiles? She'd assumed that Ludmilla's father performed the same kind of research her own father did, space medicine. Suddenly everything felt more serious—more dangerous—now that missiles had been mentioned. She felt a heaviness to the air like there was more happening than she understood.

She immediately wanted to deny that Ludmilla had ever said anything of the sort, but suddenly she wasn't certain. When they'd flipped through the American magazines, hadn't Ludmilla sometimes daydreamed about living there, visiting the candy shops with treats of all shapes and sizes, enormous shiny cars in every driveway, drinking Coca-Cola and dancing to Elvis's music?

Mama cleared her throat.

"Oh, no," Nina quickly said. "She never said anything like that."

Ivan added with conviction, "We denounce them, sir! We are loyal to the Motherland above all else."

The Chief Designer patted him on the shoulder. "Good, loyal children. You make the Motherland proud."

He left, saying a few reassuring words to Papa. Nina felt her shoulders sink in relief. It had felt like another test, and she hoped she had passed. When she turned to Ivan, she found him smiling proudly, stars in his eyes that one of the top leaders of the Communist Party had given them a compliment. There was something about the look on her brother's face that Nina didn't like at all. She was glad that he hadn't overheard the talk of missiles.

She grabbed his hand protectively. "Come on, little monster. Let's go home."

7

LAIKA

DURING HER DAYS IN THE alley, Laika had never cared much about the world of people except for learning the few words required to survive: words like *dogcatcher* and *mongrel* and *scram!* She'd never cared to get close to people, either. Why would she? The cobbler's wife had pretended to be kind once by offering her a bowl of milk, only to yell when Laika smelled the poison in it and ran. But there was something different about the girl who had given her the blue blanket. It smelled like flowers in the park, like warmer days. Such a bright blue, the blue of the sky. The blue of freedom.

"What is that thing?" Mushka yapped, and then her ears perked up. "A blanket!" She paced happily, her pink tongue lolling out. "I love blankets. Children have the best blankets. Soft ones. Warm ones." She stopped, cocking her head in puzzlement. "That one looks . . . broken."

It was true that the blanket had loose threads and a strange thick knot at one end, but Laika was used to broken things.

"I'll tell you what it is," Albina said.

Both Laika and Mushka fell silent as the old dog stood up. She stretched out her stiff muscles and lifted her chin.

"It's a promise."

Mushka whined, "Um . . . I'm pretty sure it's called a blanket."

Albina sighed. "It's *more* than a blanket. Laika, this girl selected you. She smells of one of the people in white coats. She is Whiskers's pup, his child. For her to journey here and present you with a prized token—it means something."

"What does it mean?" Laika asked, confused.

"Think about it," Albina said. "What kind of dogs have children who give them blankets?"

Laika hesitated. "Warm Dogs do."

"Exactly."

Laika felt a shift in her thinking. She blinked as the truth of it stared her in the face. Warm Dogs had children who gave them blankets. *This* girl had given her a blanket. Laika felt dazed, wary of believing it, but the old dog's logic seemed faultless.

"But I've never even seen that girl before," Laika said.

"The Dog Star doesn't bring a dog and a person together without a reason," Albina scoffed.

Laika sat back. Could it possibly be true? Could the

girl intend to make her a Warm Dog? Many thoughts pawed through her head. She hadn't believed old Albina's story before, and she was still wary of doing so, even after the girl's kindness. She sniffed the blanket. Gnawed on the bulky knot of blue thread. It felt good to chew. She thought back to the fat little dog in the window cradled by a girl in pigtails. She tried to imagine herself held in the girl's arms. But every image she pictured only turned into the cobbler's wife hurling shoes.

She scowled. "No. I don't believe it."

Albina cocked her head. "Your heart is full of doubt, little one. What if you allowed in hope instead?"

Laika hesitated, then turned away. Hope? She barely knew the word.

Mushka yawned and curled up in her crate. She began to snore, her paws chasing rabbits in her sleep, while Laika nosed her way under the blanket. It molded around her small body, tucking itself around her. She sighed, relaxing into the warmth.

Once the world beyond the window grew dark, Soft Hands came to feed them supper. When she approached Laika's cage, Laika growled a low warning, still wary. Soft Hands set the bowl of food near the door to her crate and locked the door again.

But when she went to the kitchen to refill Mushka's water dish, she left Mushka's door open. Laika sat up, alert. An open door. Mushka could escape! But Mushka only yawned and blinked awake at the smell of food and panted happily as Soft Hands returned and scratched beneath her chin.

Laika continued to watch in shock. Why hadn't Mushka tried to escape? When Soft Hands fed Albina, she left that crate door open for several minutes, too. An idea took root in Laika's head. Albina and Mushka didn't growl when the people in white coats came. They let them pet and scratch them.

Maybe if I act obedient, they'll leave my crate door open, too.

She spent the rest of the evening carefully watching how Albina and Mushka interacted with the people in white coats. They never growled. They licked the people's hands instead of biting. Mushka even rolled over to expose her belly!

Soon the other dogs were sound asleep, and only Laika remained awake in the dark parlor. She dragged over the blanket and rested her chin on the knot. It was wonderfully soft compared to the concrete of the shoe-store stoop. It smelled of the girl, of springtime. Her eyelids began to fall.

From the window, a beam of light shone down on her. She tilted her chin up at the brightest star in the night sky.

You are a long way from your stoop, the Dog Star said.

Laika blinked into the light. She asked in a quiet voice, "Is what Albina says true? If I master the tricks, will this girl make me a Warm Dog?"

What do you believe?

56

Laika rested her chin again on the blanket, thinking. "The only way to survive is alone." It had been her belief for so long that she didn't know any other way to think.

The Dog Star sparkled, sending shimmering glints dancing in Laika's eyes.

Do you know the history of dog and human?

She shook her head.

I will tell you a story. It begins on a night long ago, a night even colder than this one. Before houses. Before cars. The only light came from the stars. Wolves, your ancestors, stalked the forest for the sounds of scurrying shrews.

Laika listened in wonder.

The ancestors were led by a she-wolf named Snow. The pack hunted with quick, panting breaths. Snow stopped. Ahead, she saw a flash of light through the trees.

Laika gasped. "A fallen star?"

So Snow thought as well. There it was, crackling just beyond the trees. A wonderful smell of roasting meat reached the ancestors' noses. Tall Ones, *the wolves whispered among themselves. The creatures who dressed in fur coats with thick boots and wielded sharpened sticks. The wolf pack sensed danger and turned away despite the rich smell, but Snow stopped. Ahead, lost in the forest, was a little Tall One.*

"A human child?" Laika asked.

Yes. His face was wet with tears. His fingers were

blackening from the cold. But when his eyes met Snow's, he didn't scream. Though the other wolves warned her of the Tall Ones' dangerous ways, Snow felt pity for the lost human child, and led him by the wrist to his people's fire before disappearing back into the woods. She crept close again the next night to check on the child. This time, the fire was even larger, the smell even more savory. The Tall Ones danced around a hunk of roasting mammoth. The boy saw Snow at the edge of the forest. He didn't yell or chase her away. Instead, he tossed a bone to her. It was slick with grease and small bits of fat still in the joint. Since that day, dogs and humans have had a special bond. Dogs take care of humans, and humans take care of dogs.

"But how could they trust one another?" Laika asked.

The Dog Star's light pulsed. *Trust takes courage, little one.*

8

NINA

ON THE RIDE BACK TO Moscow, Nina's head spun. Had she given the Chief Designer the answers he wanted? Maybe she should have done more to denounce Ludmilla's family, as Ivan had. But how could she say such things when it wasn't what she believed? Ludmilla's family wasn't that different from her own. She'd dreamed of American movie stars just like Ludmilla had. And like Ludmilla's parents, her own parents sometimes whispered about the Communist Party spreading half-truths. Would the Party turn on them, too?

She reached into her pocket for the soothing touch of Ludmilla's scarf before she remembered the white dog with the chocolate-and-tan face. For some reason, giving the blue scarf to Laika had felt very urgent, very important. There was something about that dog that whispered that she needed a friend.

Even without Ludmilla's scarf, Nina still remembered every time they'd sat by her bedroom window and made up stories about the people passing by below, all the well-loved books they'd shared, all the jokes about Pyotr's gap teeth. She pressed her hand against her heart, feeling a rush of longing. Maybe Laika wasn't the only one who needed a friend.

". . . you are too much of an idealist," Mama was whispering to Papa from the front seat. "If the Chief Designer says the launch must happen, then it must happen."

"Before it is ready?"

"The premier himself insists that the rocket launch before the New Year's celebration. The Americans are working around the clock on their own rockets. He wants to show them that with a new year comes a stronger Soviet Union."

"That isn't enough time," Papa whispered back.

"You heard the warning in the Chief Designer's words. The whole world is watching. If the mission fails, you might lose your position with the Institute of Space Medicine. We could lose our home. Our reputation within the Communist Party—" Mama cut herself off, glancing at the children in the back seat. She added quietly, "You know what happens to political dissidents."

Nina drew in a sharp breath at her parents' whispered words. Had the Sokolovs talked like this? She glanced at Ivan, worried. But he was practicing tying a knot they'd learned in Young Pioneers with a bit of twine, oblivious to the conversation in the front seat.

Papa answered, "The Chief Designer did not say I would be in danger of being labeled a dissident."

Mama said quietly, "Not with words. But why do you think he wanted to question the children? That is how they divide a family. They start with the children, get them to report on their parents. Ever since Sergei Sokolov's betrayal, they've been watching all of us more closely."

The remainder of the ride was filled with silence. It was past bedtime when they got home.

When Mama came to tell her good night, Nina asked, "Can I visit the dogs again?"

"I don't think so, lapochka. Besides . . ." Mama opened the dresser. She took out a white shirt, a navy blue sweater, and a crisp red Young Pioneers kerchief. "You have other things to think of. Tomorrow there is another Young Pioneers rally after school."

Nina scowled at the red kerchief. Now that she knew the Young Pioneers had reported Ludmilla, she didn't like the look of the thing.

Mama sat on the bed, stroking Nina's hair. "You must do this, lapochka. You must attend the rally. Sing loudest. Salute the highest."

Nina clenched her jaw. "Do you tell Ivan to do the same?"

"I don't have to. Ivan only has stars in his eyes for the Party." She paused, continuing to stroke Nina's hair. "But you, my clever girl. You see more than your brother does, yes? Tomorrow, be a good girl for me. For all of us." She leaned in and whispered, "There are worse places people disappear to than America."

That night, Nina didn't sleep, tossing and turning with visions of the military police banging on their door, until her thoughts settled on the brown-and-white dog. She pictured Laika soaring to the stars while the whole world cheered. All of Russia and all of America. A girl in Moscow and a girl in Boston. Maybe this would be one thing the world could agree on: that a single small dog could change the future.

In the morning, Nina reluctantly dressed in the Young Pioneers uniform and, after a long day of classes, met Ivan on the steps after school.

"Hurry, Nina, we'll be late!"

He grabbed her mittened hand and tugged her into the courtyard, where dozens of students wearing the red kerchief were laughing and chasing one another and jumping in place to keep warm.

Director Stepko climbed to the top of the steps and clapped three times. Nina folded her arms tightly, looking away. He was supposed to lead and protect his students—how could he have turned one in? He signaled to a pair of boys, one who lifted a red flag, and the other who pressed a bugle to his lips. Nina flinched at the blare of the horn.

Ivan ran to join the fourth-year boys, where he picked up a red flag and took his place at the head of the line. Nina made her way across the yard to join her classmates.

The bugle boy tortured his instrument for a few more notes, and then Director Stepko announced, "Young Pioneers! Be prepared to fight for the cause of the Communist Party of the Soviet Union!"

"Always prepared!" the students answered in response, then began to sing.

> *"High rise our campfires into the blue night,*
> *We are pioneers—the children of the workers,*
> *Near is the time of our best years*
> *And the pioneers' motto is, 'Always be ready!'"*

Nina sang loudly, as her mother had ordered, but each word only made her more confused. *Campfires? Best years?* Where were the lines about reporting twelve-year-old girls to the authorities? The song ended abruptly, but Nina kept singing until a few kids looked over and snickered.

Director Stepko held up his hands until the crowd silenced. In a warning voice, he said, "These are uncertain times for the Motherland. Our Communist way of life is under threat. One day, you Young Pioneers might be called upon to defend our home against foreign invaders." He signaled to Ivan's group of boys, who disappeared into a storage shed. They came back out with nets and mesh bags full of big white balls. Director Stepko's face broke into a smile. "So let us practice being united as teams!"

"Pioneerball!" the girl next to Nina squealed with delight.

Ivan and the other fourth-year boys began handing out balls. The students began forming pairs. Nina stood alone. If Ludmilla had been here, there'd have been no question that they'd be partners. She spotted Tatyanna, but Tatyanna was already paired with another girl.

"Hurry, now," Director Stepko said to the crowd. "Be efficient and orderly, just like little soldiers."

Nina grimaced. She couldn't bear to look at Director Stepko any longer. He was the reason her best friend was gone, why the Chief Designer's attention was now focused on *her* family.

What if she said the wrong thing? What if she hadn't sung loudly enough?

Her stomach churned. She was breathing hard, and the air around her started to go black.

"Nina Konstantinova!" Her teacher, Olenka Ivanovna, appeared by her side. "Are you unwell?"

The courtyard continued to spin. Nina let out a moan.

Olenka Ivanovna sighed. "You are excused from Pioneerball. Go to the school cafeteria. The service project students are meeting there—you may sit with them until you feel better."

Nina's vision cleared enough for her to gratefully escape the courtyard and head inside to the cafeteria, where Assistant Director Garibov, a kind young teacher with a mop of red hair, sat around a table with a half dozen students. He waved to her with a smile and motioned to a seat. She sank into it, burying her head in her hands.

"Go on, Ana," Assistant Director Garibov said to an eighth-year girl. "Tell us about your service project."

"I've been meeting before school with students from year two who are struggling with reading," the girl said.

"I joined the volunteer fire brigade," the boy next to her said proudly. "We do drills every afternoon until supper."

"I spent every weekend this month collecting paper and scrap metal," another girl said.

The room grew quiet and Nina realized she was next.

"Oh, I'm just waiting here because I got sick during Pioneerball," she explained.

Assistant Director Garibov nodded in understanding. "Sports are not for everyone. Perhaps you might prefer to join our group of volunteers?"

Nina quickly started to shake her head; Ludmilla had been part of the Young Pioneer volunteers, working at the state orphanage, and look where it had gotten her.

But Assistant Director Garibov wasn't put off. "There are many ways to serve your Party. Do you enjoy working with the elderly? Or with the sick in the hospital?"

She didn't want to collect scrap metal or join the fire brigade. Perhaps a few months ago she would have happily tutored other students or read aloud to the elderly, but now everything felt like a trap.

Assistant Director Garibov reached out and patted her hand. "Isn't there anything you care about, Nina Konstantinova?"

She took a moment to think about this question. Ivan was happy throwing balls around and waving flags, but she never would be. She needed a safe place. She needed people she could trust—but was that possible anymore? Was there anyone she could entrust with fears, with secrets?

She felt a tingle in her chest as she remembered the little brown-and-white dog. Dogs, unlike people, would never betray her.

Nina said quietly, "Dogs."

Assistant Director Garibov's eyebrows rose as he repeated quizzically, "Dogs?"

Nina felt a rush of confidence now. She sat up straighter. "Yes, dogs. I can help my father with the dogs who will be sent into space!" She paused and added, "Through this, um, I can make the Motherland proud."

"Okay, then," the assistant director said hesitantly. "Dogs."

That night, when she told Papa her plan, he sadly shook his head. "It's impossible. Star City is a top secret facility."

"The Chief Designer allowed us to visit Star City once," Nina pressed. "He even said himself that he wants us to be good comrades, make ourselves useful."

Papa glanced at Mama above his newspaper. "What do you think, Lidia?"

Her mother had been writing correspondence and now set down her pen, frowning. Nina turned to her mother and said, "Mama, please don't make me go back to the Young Pioneer rallies." She paused and then added, "Besides, if I do a service project, it will *prove my loyalty to Russia.*"

Mama looked meaningfully at Papa. "She has a point, Konstantin."

Papa rubbed the bridge of his nose. "I suppose it would be good for the dogs to have a playmate, someone to take them for longer walks and entertain them outside their crates. We try, but we haven't the time to make their lives as enriching as we'd like."

The pull of a smile played at Nina's lips.

"All right, lapochka. Friday afternoons, instead of the Young Pioneer rallies. If the Chief Designer agrees, then you may help with the dogs."

She threw her arms around her father, who chuckled and hugged her back.

9

LAIKA

GOOD GIRL.

That was what Laika was starting to call Whiskers's child in her head. Albina had named the other humans, like Whiskers and Soft Hands. So why couldn't Laika name one? Her instinct was still to remain wary of people, but the Dog Star's stories about people and dogs helping one another had loosened the fearful knots in her heart. And the girl *had* been very good to give her the blanket.

As the sun continued to rise and fall, the people in white coats gave Laika food and water and cleaned the straw at the bottom of her cage, and a young soldier came to walk her twice a day in Star City's courtyard. She resisted the urge to growl when he leashed her. She didn't bristle when they picked her up. In return, she grew used to Albina's and Mushka's presence and even caught herself snickering at Mushka's antics. The woman they'd named Soft Hands started to leave the key in the lock of Laika's cage when she fed her, though she hadn't yet left the door open.

Laika found herself often looking toward the parlor door, hoping to see Good Girl. But then she'd scold herself and remember that despite what Albina and the Dog Star said, escape was more important. Soon the people would trust her enough to leave the crate door open. During her walks with the soldier, she'd memorized the layout of the hallways that led to the courtyard. Now all that was left was to learn how to slip the leash and collar from around her neck.

The next time the parlor door opened, Whiskers and Soft Hands came in, carrying Mushka. They'd taken her earlier in the day to practice one of the tricks, but today, something was different. Laika sniffed the air. It reeked of chemicals.

As soon as the people in white coats left, Laika whirled toward Mushka.

"What did they do to you?" Laika was surprised by the protective growl in her voice. Her eyes searched the fluffy dog for wounds or blood, and she was relieved to find none. "Are you okay? You smell afraid."

Mushka panted, "I'm never afraid!" But when Albina gave Mushka a hard look, Mushka admitted, "I was a little afraid at first, but it was only my second time in the Shake-Shake Box." She sat up as tall as she could, her chin raised proudly. "They gave me treats when I finished. I did good!"

"Did *well*," Albina muttered.

Soft Hands and Whiskers returned to the parlor with a strange glass ball. Two new men were with them. One had round spectacles and a bald head. The other was a stooped man holding a few folds of fabric. Laika sniffed the air. For a moment, she was back in the shoe-store alley.

"I smell leather."

Albina nodded. "Yes. That man with glass over his eyes is called the Hairless Leader. We call the stooped man Tailor. You know what a cobbler does, yes? Stitches the things people wear on their feet? Tailor stitches in much the same way. Clothes to protect the head and body. But Tailor makes clothes for *us*."

Laika swiped her paw dismissively. "Dogs don't wear clothes."

"Starflyers do."

Soft Hands unlocked Laika's cage. Laika tensed but reminded herself not to growl.

Soft Hands slid her palm to cradle Laika's chest and gently lifted her. Tailor approached her with outstretched hands and she bristled, but he only scratched her chin kindly.

Laika couldn't stop her legs from trembling as Soft Hands set her on a worktable. She glanced at the freedom beyond the window. The blue sky had been replaced with signs of a coming storm.

Tailor stretched a long piece of white tape from her chest to her tail, then from the top of her shoulders to the tops of her front feet. He measured the tape over the leather fabric, too, then nodded. He gently lifted each of Laika's feet and slid her paws through holes in the fabric, first the left-back, then right-back, left-front, right-front. Shoe leather was stiff, but this leather was buttery soft and fit snugly against her chest.

Act obedient, she told herself. *Win their trust.*

So she didn't squirm when Soft Hands stroked her back. She didn't bare her teeth. Laika realized that, though the starflyer clothing felt strange, the fabric expanded and contracted comfortably with each breath. Soon she'd almost forgotten she was even wearing it.

Tailor fastened leather straps around Laika's body, then stepped back. The people in white coats seemed to come to some sort of agreement, and Soft Hands picked up the big glass bowl. She carefully lowered it over Laika's head. It matched up with a metal ring at the top of her dog-clothes. The people fumbled with the glass orb for a few minutes. Something went *click*, and they all stepped back with smiles big enough to show their teeth.

Soft Hands carried her through the parlor door. Her heartbeat leaped as she wondered if she'd also return shaking and smelling of chemicals, as Mushka had. They took her to a room where Whiskers stood beside a box attached to lots of wires.

Soft Hands set her in the box and clipped two chains to her harness. With the heavy glass orb over her head, her neck muscles were starting to strain. Whiskers screwed a pipe to the orb and fresh air rushed in. Laika filled her lungs anxiously.

She heard some clicks and felt a jolt—without warning, the box moved!

It began as a low rumble, like a big truck had rolled by. Vibrations traveled up Laika's legs. She lifted one paw, then another. The vibrations increased. Now her legs were trembling, and she had to sway back and forth to steady herself. Once, an apartment building near the shoe store had caught fire and collapsed in on itself, and the whole earth had shaken violently. The box shook just as hard now. The vibrations were making her stomach twist. Air continued to flow through the glass orb, but it tasted stale now.

Whiskers turned up a dial and the box shook harder. Laika's tongue lolled out of her mouth, dripping saliva. Her vision grew jumbled. Then she arranged her thoughts:

This must be the Shake-Shake Box. Albina did it. Mushka did it. So I can do it, too.

Laika pulled her tongue back into her mouth. Aware that the people in white coats were watching her, she fought against the roiling feeling in her stomach. She dug in her nails to steady herself. She focused on a black bolt on the side of the Shake-Shake Box, and her vision centered itself.

After a few minutes, the people in white coats clicked off the machine.

Soft Hands detached the glass orb from around her

neck. It caught on her skull and Laika couldn't imagine that they'd ever get it off, but then Soft Hands gently guided Laika's head back and to the side, and she slipped out of the orb easily. Laika sucked in big gulps of fresh air.

The people in white coats were nodding excitedly.

When they returned her to the parlor, the storm had picked up outside. Freezing rain pelted the window. If she were back in her alley, she would wait out the miserable storm in her crate, hungry and alone. She was surprised by how happy she was to return to the familiar smells of Albina and Mushka, to a warm crate, to safety from the storm.

Soft Hands gave her a pat and filled her bowl, and then the scientists left and switched off the main lights. Only the lamp on the old fireplace stayed illuminated, as well as the blinking machinery on the other side of the room. A few stars appeared beyond the window.

Laika thrust forward to gulp down the food, but in place of the usual sausage, there was only a single dollop of gelatinous goo. It was clear and wobbly, though it *smelled* like meat. Laika recoiled, eyeing the substance suspiciously. "This isn't food!"

Albina chuckled under her breath. "The texture takes getting used to. This is what they feed us in the rockets, so they want us to practice eating it."

After a tentative bite of the goo, Laika discovered it wasn't as bad as she'd feared. Better than shoe leather and bony mice, in any case. It had been a long time since she'd felt that old yawning hunger in her belly. Her muscles had filled out, grown strong. Her wounds had healed with the help of the people's salves.

"Mushka?" she said. She wasn't certain the other dogs were still awake.

The fluffy dog yawned. "Yes?"

Laika shifted on Good Girl's blanket. "I'm glad you're okay."

"You too, my friend!"

Laika's body tensed. *Friend?* Friends were dogs you trusted, dogs you hunted with. She'd never had a friend. But as she chewed on the corner of the blanket, she thought that if she did have a pack, she supposed she wouldn't mind if Mushka and Albina were part of it. It didn't mean she would stay at Star City, though. It was only a matter of time before she'd go through with her escape.

And now, another piece of the puzzle was in place. When Soft Hands had shown Laika how to get her head out of the glass orb, she had also inadvertently taught her how to slip her collar and leash.

Laika rested her head on the knot at the end of the blue blanket. For a moment, she dared to wonder if Albina's promise could be true. Would Good Girl return? If she did, maybe Laika wouldn't need to go through with the escape. Maybe something better could be waiting at the end.

10

NINA

NINA THREW OPEN THE DOOR that led from the Institute of Space Medicine's kitchen to the parlor. Every day that week she had daydreamed about scratching furry ears instead of waving flags. Singing the dogs rock 'n' roll songs instead of Soviet anthems. Playing fetch in the courtyard instead of Pioneerball. A few moments of peace with animals who didn't question her loyalty to the Party.

"Nina, wait!" Svetlana Popovich called after her as she headed directly into the parlor. "First I must show you how to prepare their food dishes . . ."

But Nina was too excited. A grin spread across her face as she went to Laika's cage and wove her fingers between the bars.

"Hello, troublemaker. Did you think I wouldn't be back?"

The brown-and-white dog hung back, but her tail started wagging.

Nina dug into her pocket. "Look what I brought for you." She pulled out a napkin with a bit of leftover chicken breast from last night's dinner. She pushed the meatiest scrap between the bars and Laika snapped it up, went over to the blue scarf, curled up, and started eating, pausing between bites to look up at Nina curiously.

The fluffy dog in the next cage started barking excitedly.

Nina laughed. "Okay, Mushka. I brought one for you, too." She passed another piece of leftover chicken through the bars to Mushka, and then one to Albina.

Svetlana shook her head, though she was smiling. "Those dogs are going to get lazy if you baby them like that," she scolded. "Was it you who gave that scrap of blue fabric to Laika? You'd think she'd had it forever. She curls up with it each night. Carries it around with her wherever she goes. We tried to take it from her when we took her out to weigh her, but she growled at us until we let her keep it. Sometimes dogs develop an attachment to an object, just like people do."

Nina's eyes fell on Ludmilla's tattered scarf, well-chewed by enthusiastic dog teeth.

Svetlana handed her two leather leashes. "Mushka is scheduled to train in the centrifuge today, so you may take Laika and Albina for a walk in the courtyard. Exercise and fresh air will be good for them. But remember that you aren't here to play. The dogs are our colleagues and we must treat them as such. Their work is just as important as any human cosmonaut's."

Nina blinked a few times before she took the leashes. It hadn't occurred to her to think of the dogs as *colleagues*, as crucial to the mission's success as the scientists. She realized that because of these ordinary dogs, one day the world might watch a person fly to outer space, even land on the moon. She felt herself grinning that she might be a small part of that.

"I understand," she told Svetlana.

She leashed both dogs and led them down the long hallway to a door where a soldier stood at attention.

"I'm supposed to take the dogs for a walk," Nina said.

He glanced at the dogs sniffing his boots. "You can let Albina off the leash. The old girl won't bolt. But be careful with that one." He nodded toward Laika. "She'll disappear on you when she thinks you aren't looking."

He unlocked the door, and Nina led the dogs into the courtyard. It was a bright day, but the sun wasn't strong enough to melt the snow that padded the courtyard a foot thick. The courtyard was surrounded on all sides by the curved walls of the palace, with its turrets and crumbling columns. The only opening was a gate at the far end that led to the street, where the military trucks entered and exited. It was blocked by a tall fence and soldiers with guns.

Nina let the dogs sniff the bushes that lined the

shoveled pathway. Albina nosed around tiny tracks that hinted at the presence of mice. But Laika stayed close to Nina, peering up at her with the blue scarf clenched in her jaw, that same curious look in her eyes.

Nina sat on a bench and patted her lap. "Come on, troublemaker. You want a scratching, is that it?"

Laika hesitated, but then jumped into her lap. She curled into a tight ball and rested her head on Nina's wrist. The warm, soft weight in her lap made Nina smile. Laika's tail began to wag slowly as Nina gently petted her back. She frowned as she felt old scars beneath the fur, and evidence of bones that had broken and healed unevenly.

"I wish you could tell me what adventures you've had," Nina murmured. "How did such a little thing survive out there on your own?"

Laika tucked her head close to Nina's coat and closed her eyes.

Nina reached into her satchel. "I brought a present for you. This is a story my brother and I loved when we were little. It's called 'The Firebird and the Gray Wolf.' I thought you'd like it because wolves aren't that different from dogs. You might not understand words, but I'm guessing you can make sense of pictures."

She opened the book and began to read while pointing to the pictures. When she flipped to a picture of a wolf with a prince riding on its back, Laika's ears perked up.

"Ah!" Nina laughed. "You understand, after all?"

"The Firebird and the Gray Wolf" was about a prince on a quest for a golden firebird. He was left helpless when a wolf killed and ate his horse, so instead he befriended and rode on the wolf. The prince and the wolf together avenged wrongs and won battles and rescued a princess. It was a marvelous story of a person and an animal working as one.

For a while Laika stared at the drawings intently, but then she yawned and leaned into Nina's chest. Slowly, her eyes began to close.

Nina shut the book and returned to gently scratching the dog while Albina sniffed around the bushes on the other side of the courtyard.

"Papa says the newspaper is about to print a long article about the Starflyer mission. And that newspapers in other countries will print the story, too. Soon the whole world will know about you dogs. You'll be more famous than Marilyn Monroe!"

Laika began breathing heavily, almost asleep.

Nina looked up at the dark clouds overhead. "They'll probably even hear news of the Starflyer mission in Boston." She paused, looking over her shoulder, but the guards were too far away to hear her. It was only her and Laika. Nina continued hesitantly, "I had a friend once. A best friend. That scarf you've got there, that belonged to her. Everyone tells me I have to keep her secret and pretend like she never existed, but she did. And now she's gone and I can't just act like everything is the same."

Laika opened her eyes, looking steadily at Nina. Nina couldn't help but feel like the little dog, somehow, on some level, heard her.

She hugged the little dog close. "You'll keep my secrets."

Laika rested a paw on Nina's hand.

They stayed like that until the young soldier opened the door again, calling to her that it was time to fetch Albina and bring the two dogs back inside. Once they were back in the parlor, Nina returned the dogs to their crates and found Svetlana in the kitchen.

"Are you sure Laika didn't belong to a family?" she asked.

Svetlana finished weighing a bowl of dog food and set it on the counter. "Laika? She was definitely a stray. We found her living in a wooden crate next to a shoe store in an alley across the street from Winter Park. She was badly malnourished and wounded—I think she'd been in a fight with other dogs."

Nina glanced back at the dogs in their crates. "What will happen to them after the mission? To the one who flies in the rocket and to the ones who aren't chosen?"

"Well, Albina is getting old. If she isn't chosen for this mission, then she'll be retired. Dimitri—one of the junior scientists—has already asked if he can adopt her when it is time. All the dogs are adopted when they retire."

"What about Laika? She deserves a home after her mission."

"Of course she does."

Nina hesitated. "Maybe Papa would let me adopt her."

Svetlana gave a gentle smile. "You'll have to talk to him about that. In the meantime, here." She handed Nina a scoop and a pair of gloves with a glint of mischief in her eyes. "You wanted to contribute to the Communist Party, right? There is great nobility in manual labor."

Nina groaned as she took the scoop and headed for the courtyard to clean up after the dogs.

11

LAIKA

SEVERAL DAYS PASSED, AND LAIKA kept thinking about that afternoon with Good Girl, about the pieces of chicken and the back scratches and the book with the pictures of amazing things, of people riding on the backs of wolves. Maybe the Dog Star *had* sent Good Girl to Laika for a reason, as Albina had said. In the Dog Star's story, the wolf named Snow had been very brave, brave enough to approach a human child, and the child had been kind to the wolf in return. So maybe if Laika wanted Good Girl to keep coming back with more chicken and back scratches, *she* would have to be brave. *She* would have to be a good girl.

So when Soft Hands carried her down dark hallways to a large, strange building filled with odd machinery, she resisted her instinct to squirm or growl.

I must do this for Good Girl, she thought.

The structure smelled unlike the rest of Star City. Laika sniffed harder, then it came to her: *horses*. That was the smell. Like the ones in Moscow that had kicked her when she nosed their feed bags. But there weren't any horses here now. The building was a high-ceiling structure with hay dusting the floor and partitions along one wall.

The word drifted into her head: *stable*.

She'd once snuck into a stable built beneath the city streets, but that one had been dank and overcrowded with animals. This one was full of fresh air. On top of the lingering smell of horses floated the newer scents of chemicals and motor oil. In the center of the stable towered a machine as tall as a person, with two metal arms reaching out, each holding a wire basket just big enough for a small dog.

Whiskers sat at a desk, scratching at paper with a wooden stick. He looked up and nodded to Soft Hands. Tailor held a shiny round object in the palm of his hand with ticking parts turning in a steady circle.

Soft Hands set Laika on the desk and held her steady while Tailor pressed a piece of metal to her chest. She flinched against the cold. He wound a strip of cloth around the metal to hold it in place, and then the machine started beeping in time with Laika's heart. On the machine, thin wire arms scratched out wavy lines on paper.

Soft Hands placed her inside one of the wire baskets and strapped her down with a piece of leather. Whiskers said something to Tailor, who flipped a lever on the wall. A heavy *clank* rang out. The basket lurched forward. It spun slowly at first, no faster than Laika could walk, but Laika crouched low anyway, digging her nails in to steady herself. The basket started moving faster in a circle. The clanking of the machinery grew louder. The people in white coats shouted to one another over the noise. Whiskers, at the desk, watched the machinery and continued to scratch at his paper. The machine beeped faster and faster as the speed picked up. Wind ruffled Laika's ears. She narrowed her eyes to keep them from watering. The room was soon moving so fast that everything became a smear of colors. She pressed herself to the cage bottom. The wind made it difficult to breathe. Some unseen force pushed her to the side of the basket.

Like a storm, she thought to herself. *This must be the Spinning Storm!*

She was used to bolting in the face of danger, but here there was no place to go. She whined, but no one came to her aid. The machine only spun faster.

The last time she'd felt this rush of fear had been in the alley, faced with the old black dog and the brindle and the lanky pup. *I didn't back down then*, she thought. *I won't back down now.* She forced her eyes open. Found that even with the screeching wind, she could breathe if she took small, shallow breaths. She braced herself against the bottom of the basket, and the sick feeling in her stomach lessened. She kept her head low, leaning into the wind instead of fighting it.

Was this like flying? For a moment, she imagined this

was what it felt like to be the Dog Star, spinning and spinning on top of the world.

Almost as soon as it had started, the machine slowed. The mysterious force pushing Laika to the side lessened, and she could sit upright again. Her heartbeat slowed, as did the machine's beeping. At last, the wire basket stopped.

The people in white coats were talking excitedly. They huddled around the paper with the squiggly lines. After a few minutes, Soft Hands took Laika out of the basket and proudly held her up toward the ceiling. The people in white coats cheered. But now that she'd stopped spinning, Laika felt a lurch in her stomach. When Soft Hands set her on the ground, she found that she couldn't walk straight.

The people in white coats were huddled around the desk, speaking loudly among themselves. Laika tried to take another step, only to stumble.

Two hands caught her before she fell.

Whiskers swept her up into his arms. Laika blinked up at him, this man who smelled so much like Good Girl.

Tell her, Laika thought. *Tell her that I was brave.*

12

NINA

NINA DREW HER COAT TIGHTER around her as she squinted up at the street signs. The snow was falling more heavily now, turning the world white. She paused beneath the awning of an apartment building and pulled out the map she'd taken from her mother's desk, tracing her finger along the roads until she found Winter Park.

She refolded the map with numb fingers and, looking both ways, jogged across the snow-covered street.

It had been nearly a week since her last visit to the Institute of Space Medicine, and she'd kept thinking about Laika and wondering what her life had been like before the Institute. So after school while Mama took Ivan to the barber, Nina snuck out to the place where Svetlana had found Laika.

Finally, the park gates loomed in the falling snow. Nina hugged her coat, looking around for a shoe store. She had to circle the park twice before she found it tucked beside an alleyway, easy to overlook. A small, run-down place with a pair of boots painted on the front door and a sign swinging in the storm: KOKORIN COBBLERS.

She pushed back her hood and stepped into the alley, where the wind blew a little less. Immediately she pressed her mitten against her nose. The alley reeked of freshly tanned leather and strong glue. It was overrun with garbage that didn't seem to be picked up very often, judging by the mess. Hesitantly, Nina poked around until she found a broken crate about the right size for a small dog to sleep in. She crouched to look inside. A few rags in the bottom. Some tiny old bones, probably once belonging to a mouse. White fur matted in the rags.

Her heart sank.

Despite what Svetlana had said, Nina had hoped to find a cozy little box, sturdy and warm, or else a family that had once loved Laika. But this sad place told a story of a dog who had lived a hard, cold life.

Nina climbed the steps and knocked on the shoe store's rear entrance. After a moment, the door swung open to reveal the pinched face of a woman who might have been pretty if she'd had an easier life.

She eyed Nina's fine boots, brand-new and not in need of repair. "If you're looking for the cobbler, use the front entrance."

"Oh, I'm not here about shoes." Nina motioned to the alley. "I want to ask about a dog that might have lived here.

A little brown-and-white dog? Maybe with a bit of husky in her?"

The woman's face pulled into a sour expression. "What could you possibly want with that dirty stray?"

Nina flinched to hear Laika referred to as dirty. "Oh . . . I thought she might have been your pet?"

The woman coughed a laugh. "Not likely. We tried everything to get rid of her. Poisoned food. Traps. She was a wily one. We called the dogcatcher a dozen times, but she always managed to make herself scarce when he showed up. Something must have gotten her in the end. We haven't seen her in a while. Why, did she belong to you? No, I can't imagine she did. She's been out there for going on a year without a soul to claim her. Not the kind of dog anyone would ever want."

Nina narrowed her eyes. She shook her head fiercely. "No one would want her? You're wrong. That 'dirty stray' might soon become the most famous dog in the world, a space dog. The whole world is going to know her. Just wait and see."

She stomped away before the surprised woman could respond.

As she made her way home, she promised herself that Laika would never go back to life in the alley. And she couldn't return to her old life, either, she realized, back to days with Ludmilla and magazines and essays about the great Motherland—not when she wasn't sure anymore if it *was* so great.

The only path for both of them was forward.

To the launch.

As soon as Friday came, she climbed out of Mama's car at the Institute of Space Medicine, calling back over her shoulder that she would get a ride home with Papa. Warm sausage biscuits were in her pocket as she headed down the echoing old palace hallways to the dog training area.

She threw open the parlor door, only to have her smile fade when she saw that Laika's cage was empty. She found Svetlana in one of the laboratories and asked, bewildered, "Where's Laika?"

Svetlana looked up from a weight chart she was entering notations into. "You just missed her. Your father placed her inside the isolation chamber a few minutes ago."

Nina's shoulders sank. "How long will she be in there?"

"Seven days," Svetlana answered without looking up.

"Seven days!" Nina gasped. A full week locked in the darkness with no walks or glimpses of sky? The scientists were no better than the shoemakers! She stomped her foot. "You can't do that to her!"

Svetlana set down her notepad. "Nina, none of us wish to hurt or scare the dogs. But conditions in the rocket will be difficult: extreme temperatures, strong vibrations, loud sounds. The more we can do here on Earth to prepare them for the challenge, the greater chance for success they will have." Svetlana patted her shoulder. "Look at Albina." She motioned to the white dog's crate. "This old girl has been launched twice. Both times she came back to us, wagging her tail when we unhooked her from her parachute."

"But this launch goes all the way into orbit, much farther than Albina's ever did."

Svetlana nodded solemnly. "That is why we are here every day and night, putting ourselves and these dogs through so many trials. To do our best not to make any errors. We have great respect for them, just as we do for the humans who are also training to become starflyers. Each day, in a different sector of this same facility, young men sit in a tiny capsule for twenty hours at a time, did you know that? To track their ability to withstand isolation. They undergo painful tests of starvation and oxygen deprivation. They go through very similar centrifuges and simulators as these dogs."

"Why do they do it, if it hurts?"

Svetlana rested a hand on her shoulder. "Have you ever wanted something so badly that you would do whatever it took?"

Had she? Most of her life she'd gotten what she wanted, at least the important things—a bedroom of her own, books to read, the trip to the circus. Now the only thing missing in her life was Ludmilla. But there was no getting Ludmilla back. If she wanted anything now, it was answers. Why America was so bad, why her parents seemed so afraid . . .

She swallowed and asked, "Have you decided which dog will go to space? I hope it's Laika."

Svetlana squeezed her shoulder. "The results of the isolation chamber test she is in now will largely be the determining factor." She leaned in and whispered, "Between you and me, I, too, hope Laika is the one."

13

LAIKA

LAIKA TRIED TO KEEP HER limbs from trembling. Everything was blacker than the darkest winter night. The box that Whiskers had placed her in had thick walls and not a single window. The only thing inside was a receptacle of the gelatinous goo. How long had she been here? Without the rise and fall of the sun, or the routine of walks and meals, she had lost all sense of time.

She had to be in the Black Eternity. The third and final trick. Albina had warned her that this was the hardest one of all. Not as jarring as the Shake-Shake Box, not fast like the Spinning Storm, but scarier in a different way. A place of darkness, questions, and fears.

Before Whiskers had put her in here, Tailor had fastened a harness over her rump with a canvas bag attached to the end. It felt uncomfortable to have it rub against her bottom, but no matter how she scratched, she hadn't been able to get it off. Soft Hands checked her food dish, then Whiskers had sealed her in the darkness.

Laika told herself to be a good girl and to be brave, as she'd been in the Shake-Shake Box and the Spinning Storm. She'd waited anxiously for vibrations or spinning, but this box never moved. The people in white coats didn't study her with their paper and scratching sticks. There were no blinking lights. No beeping buttons.

Nothing but Laika.

The box was just big enough for her to curl up in, so she did, and waited. The walls of the box were so thick she couldn't hear or smell anything outside it. After some time, her haunches started to get tired of sitting, and she stood up, pacing in a tight circle.

Eventually, after what felt like forever, she managed to fall asleep.

When she woke, groggy, she was still in the box.

How much time had passed? Hours? An entire day? She wondered if Albina and Mushka had already been served supper. Had the people in white coats forgotten about her? What about Good Girl? Good Girl wouldn't let them keep her here forever, would she?

As more time passed, she started to feel an urge in her bowels. She usually went to the bathroom on one of the daily walks in the courtyard, but no one came to take her out. She circled the box, whining low. The bag attached to the harness dragged behind her bottom. *Oh*, she realized. She was supposed to go *in* the bag! She decided to hold it as long as she could. The people surely wouldn't keep her in here much longer. Eventually, someone would come.

But hours passed and no one did. She let out a lonely howl. "Is anyone there?"

In the darkness, a voice answered with a shimmer like a falling star.

I am always with you, little one, even if you cannot see my glow.

Laika wagged her tail. "Have the people forgotten about me?"

The Dog Star responded. *No, little one. This is why the third trick is the hardest of all. It is only you and the darkness.*

"I've survived my whole life by being alone. I'm used to it."

Do you still feel that way? Has your life not changed?

Laika considered this. *Was* she alone anymore? She'd grown so used to the companionship of Albina and Mushka. How empty the parlor felt whenever they were gone on walks or off practicing tricks. And how full of life it was when they were there. And most of all, when Good Girl came to visit.

Laika considered this for some time, then barked, "If dogs and people have a responsibility to one another, why do people chase and cage us?"

Some people are kind, some people are cruel. Some dogs are kind, some dogs are cruel. But it is

only through kindness that the world becomes a bet-
ter place for all. And kindness, as you know, takes far
more courage.

Laika thought back to the pictures in the book Good Girl had read to her. "Did the ancestors ever let people ride on their backs like a horse?"

The voice shimmered like the Dog Star was chuckling. *Only in fairy tales. But there are real tales of real dogs who have braved the worst to help people. Do you know the story of Balto?*

Laika shook her head.

Once, in a snowy land even colder than Russia, a small village was overtaken with sickness. They were too far from any cities to get medicine. So a husky named Balto led a dogsled team for many miles through treacherous terrain to deliver the medicine that would save the people in his village.

"Did they throw shoes at him?"

No, little one. He is honored among people through-out the world as a hero, as are other special dogs. Gan-der, who gave his life to save soldiers. Hachikō, who never left his master's side, even sleeping beside his grave. Mancs, who sniffed out people trapped beneath rubble.

Laika scratched her belly. "That doesn't sound like any people I've known."

One day, they will honor you, too.

Laika raised her ears at this. After years of being stalked

95

by the dogcatcher and hurt by the cobbler's family, what did she owe people? Why should she care if they honored her? But something pulled in her stomach. That hunger for something more than food. For many days she had wanted to escape Star City, but now the idea of returning to a broken shoe crate felt bleak. Especially when she thought of Good Girl, of the dream of one day being a Warm Dog.

As the Black Eternity stretched on, she closed her eyes and remembered what it looked like when the stars made their slow trot across the night sky, and thought of what it would feel like to join them up there in that midnight-blue wilderness.

14

NINA

AS OLENKA IVANOVNA WROTE THE dates of the
Bolshevik Revolution on the chalkboard at the front of
the classroom, Nina bent over her desk, drawing a picture
of Laika in a space suit. At last, Friday had come. Two
weeks had passed since she'd last seen Laika, and though
her father assured her that Laika was doing well in the
isolation chamber, she wanted to be there herself when
Laika emerged from the chamber, waiting with sausage
and a head scratch.

Nina flipped over her paper and started drawing a picture of Laika peeking out of a round spaceship window on
her way to the moon. Her white-furred chin was bravely
tipped up toward the stars.

"Nina!" Olenka Ivanovna frowned at her from the
front of the room. "Are you writing down these dates?"

Nina quickly hid her drawings. "Yes."

She spent the rest of their history lesson daydreaming that Laika would be the chosen dog and all of Moscow would attend a parade for her when she returned to Earth. When the bell rang to signal lunch break, the other students jumped up excitedly.

"Your team is going to lose," Pyotr said to Tatyanna.

"Not a chance!" Tatyanna answered.

Nina groaned out loud. As a special "treat," the Young Pioneers were playing a scouting game during lunch period, when she had no excuse to be absent. The other children were buzzing with excitement—the game, called War, was usually reserved for the upper years, since it dealt with military strategy, but in an attempt to boost Party pride, Director Stepko had granted permission for the younger students to play.

The boys in her class grabbed their coats and rushed outside. Tatyanna stopped at her desk. "Aren't you coming, Nina?"

"Do we have a choice?"

Tatyanna laughed. "No. We don't." Then her face grew serious. She leaned closer and said quietly, "I've been meaning to tell you. It wasn't nice that Pyotr tore up Ludmilla's scarf like he did."

Nina remembered that Ludmilla and Tatyanna had lived in the same apartment building. She wondered if she wasn't the only one who felt the loss of Ludmilla. No one ever talked about the Sokolov family, but that didn't mean that they were entirely forgotten. She felt a moment of hope that, amid so much secrecy, some of the secrets might be *good*.

"Nothing Pyotr does is nice," Nina answered, and Tatyanna grinned.

They dressed in their coats and hats and mittens and helped each other retie their red Young Pioneer kerchiefs around their upper arms instead of around their necks. Nina's boots sank into inches of snow as she trudged behind the other Young Pioneers into the park across the street.

"Nina Konstantinova." Director Stepko's voice rang out sharply. "Stay with the others."

She clenched her jaw. How badly she wanted to scold him for reporting on Ludmilla, for tearing her best friend away from her, but she forced her face to remain calm.

"Yes, School Director."

He nodded as she caught up with the group.

In the center of the park was a statue of five factory workers, three men and two women, who proudly displayed their hammers as a symbol of common, hardworking citizens. Snow was piled on their heads like little white hats.

Director Stepko took his place at the base of the statue.

"Pyotr. Vlad." He pointed to two of the boys. "You will be our generals."

The boys tried to hide their proud smiles as they came to stand next to him, holding their heads high.

"Years three, five, and seven will form the Soviet team. Years four, six, and eight will be the Americans." A few students groaned, including Pyotr, who, as a sixth year, was now general of the Americans. No one ever wanted to play the part of the Americans in the scouting games.

Director Stepko continued, "This game will teach you important tactical lessons. One day, you may be called upon to defend your country. These are uncertain times, and any day American missiles may come raining down from the skies. We must be prepared." He looked at each of the students' faces. "The boundary for our game is the fence around the park. Your teachers and I will be there, keeping score. The Soviet team will take the north side, the Americans the south. Each team must display their flag prominently. Boys, you will be our soldiers. Pull off another boy's kerchief and he 'dies.' Girls, you will play the part of field nurses, in charge of escorting 'dead' soldiers from the field to the 'hospital' here at the statue, where you may retie their kerchief, and they may rejoin the game. But be careful not to lose your own kerchief."

Nina shifted from one foot to the other, breathing warmth into her mittened hands. She glanced at Pyotr, who was trying to hide the smirk on his face at being named a general—even if it was for the enemy side.

Director Stepko patted Pyotr and Vlad on the shoulder. "Ready, generals?"

"Yes, comrade!" they answered in unison.

Director Stepko went to stand with the other teachers behind the safety of the park fence.

Pyotr and Vlad shook hands, then Vlad turned to his team. "Soviets, ready your ammunition!"

"Americans," Pyotr called. "Do the same!"

The boys around Nina started forming tightly packed snowballs. They stuffed as many as they could in their coat pockets. Nina crouched down to make a snowball, too.

"Not us," Tatyanna whispered. "We're field nurses, not soldiers."

"So what do we do?"

Tatyanna pointed to where the other girls were sitting on the steps at the base of the statue. "Wait for our team's soldiers to die, then we rescue them."

Nina wrinkled her nose. The last thing she wanted to do was rescue the boys in her class. She and Tatyanna tromped to the statue and took a seat.

Once the teams were in position, the generals looked to Director Stepko, who blew a whistle.

"Begin War!"

With battle yells, the teams ran across the park toward each other. Nina jumped as snowballs began flying through the air over her head. The other nurses shrieked and ducked. Boys took shelter behind trees and bushes, hurling snowballs like grenades at the opposite team. One bold boy on the Soviet team darted into American territory and was immediately pummeled with snowballs. He fell to his knees and a trio of American soldiers rushed him and ripped off the kerchief around his arm.

"You're dead!" a boy yelled.

Two of the nurses from the Soviet team jumped up. They ran to escort the fallen soldier back to the statue, but American soldiers tried to rip off their kerchiefs, too. The girls shrieked and dodged them. One managed to clutch the fallen soldier's hand and race back to the statue. Beaming, she retied the boy's kerchief around his arm.

He gave a solemn nod of thanks. "Nurse Yelena."

She nodded back. "Comrade Feliks."

Nina rolled her eyes so hard she nearly fell over backward.

A rogue snowball suddenly smashed into her belly and she doubled over, the wind knocked out of her.

Tatyanna frowned. "Pyotr threw that."

Nina narrowed her eyes, searching the battlefield for Pyotr. She wished nurses *were* allowed to hurl snowballs.

As War raged on, more and more soldiers fell, and soon all the nurses were racing into battle to stage rescue operations. Nina crawled between the legs of the stone factory workers, where she was shielded from snowballs.

"Nina!"

She jumped at the sound of her name. Olenka Ivanovna was waving to her from where the teachers stood at the side of the park. "Come here!"

Nina crawled out from under the statue. All around her, fallen boys were being escorted to the statue under a hail of snowballs. Boys were chasing other boys, pulling off their kerchiefs. A few glum-looking girls sat at the statue, their red kerchiefs missing. When a field nurse "died," apparently she died for good.

"Yes, Olenka Ivanovna?"

"You are the only nurse not working. Your soldiers need you."

Nina felt a bubble of anger rise in her throat. What if she didn't want to defend some stupid soldiers? What if she thought War was a pointless exercise, that there were other ways to deal with rivals besides battle?

Nina clenched her jaw. "Okay."

Her teacher prodded Nina toward War.

A boy cried out as another one pulled off his kerchief. She recognized him as Dima from her class. Sighing, she trudged toward where he lay dying in the snow. A Soviet soldier ran by her, reaching for her kerchief, and she jerked her arm away just in time. A snowball pelted her in the hip. She groaned and ran the rest of the way.

"Are you here to save me, Nurse Nina?" Dima asked in dramatized gasps.

"What does it look like? Come on."

She pulled him up. They ducked snowballs hurled from a Soviet battlement set up behind a nearby bush.

Dima grabbed her hand. "This way. We have to use evasive maneuvers or we'll never make it to the hospital!"

He pulled Nina behind a tree, then made her crouch down and crawl behind a row of benches. Snow had somehow gotten into her boots. Her toes were numb. Another snowball smacked her in the back of the head, and she scowled.

Dima motioned for her to stay low. "Look over there. The Soviets set up a trap. They made it look like there's a clear path to the hospital, but there's a spy hiding behind the monument plaque. We'll run for the hospital, but when you reach the plaque, make a quick turn right to dodge him."

"What will you do?"

He said bravely, "I'll let him catch me. It's a distraction technique so that you can get by him. Don't worry about me. I can get away from him again. It's only Fedya. He's a third year."

Nina shrugged.

"Right. On the count of three. One. Two. Three!"

Dima darted out, dragging Nina with him, though technically she was the one who was supposed to be escorting him. A few Soviet soldiers yelled at them. A snowball hit Nina in the back of the neck and she shuddered as ice ran down the inside of her coat.

"Now!" Dima yelled, dodging right.

Nina didn't dodge. She let go of his hand and stopped running altogether. Dima skidded to a stop and looked back at her in bewilderment.

The spy jumped out from behind the monument plaque and ripped off her kerchief. "You're dead!" he declared.

Nina took her kerchief back from him and stuffed it in her pocket. "Good."

Dima looked crestfallen. "You were supposed to dodge." His face shifted to anger. "You didn't even try."

She shrugged again and started toward the statue, where she could wait out the rest of War, until a snowball slammed into her cheek. Pain exploded across her cheekbone. She looked up to find Pyotr glaring at her.

"A deserter!" he cried. "Comrades, she's not playing by the rules. She's an enemy to Mother Russia!"

Nina clutched her aching cheek. When she looked down at the broken snowball, she found that Pyotr had mixed rocks with the snow and there were marks of blood on her mitten. Anger flared in her chest. "We're playing on the American team—of course we're the enemies of Russia, that's the whole point!"

Pyotr's face burned red. "That isn't what I meant." He raised himself up. "I think you're a *real* enemy of the people. Just like your best friend was."

A pair of field nurses gasped.

Nina felt the cold deep in her bones. Mama hadn't even wanted her to keep Ludmilla's scarf because it tied her to a traitor. What would her parents do if they learned her classmates were accusing her of betrayal to her face?

The soldiers of both teams stopped chasing one another. Pyotr pointed an accusatory finger at her. "Do you know what we do to deserters?"

Nina's cheek stung. The remnants of the snowball had melted into icy water now soaking her clothes. Tears were beginning to appear at her eyes. She looked around, her eyes settling on Ivan. Her brother would help her. But he looked confused, his head swiveling between Nina and Pyotr.

"Death by firing squad!" Pyotr announced.

Boys from both teams started hurling rock-packed snowballs. A few girls broke their roles and threw snowballs, too. Nina shrieked and rolled into a ball.

Behind a nearby bush, someone called out to her in a loud whisper, "Nina!"

She peeked out from between her fingers. "Ivan?"

"Tell them you were wrong," her brother urged. "Denounce Ludmilla."

She shook her head. "Ivan, get out of here or you'll be hurt as well."

"Nina, please," he pleaded. "If you don't denounce them . . . I have to denounce you."

She stared at him as snowballs flew overhead. Students were taught in school and Young Pioneers to put the Communist Party above family, but no one actually believed that, did they?

Then she saw the snowball in his hand.

Her stomach went cold.

"Ludmilla never did anything wrong, Ivan. I haven't, either."

He closed his eyes, grimacing. "I'm sorry." He threw the snowball in her direction. He didn't throw it as hard as the others did, but somehow, that snowball hurt the most.

More grenades of snow pounded her back and arms. She heard the teachers yelling, but it wasn't until Director Stepko stomped into the middle of War and blew a sharp whistle that the boys finally stopped.

"Students, that's quite enough!" He stepped in front of Nina. "Nina," he said sternly. "Go wait out the rest of the game with Olenka Ivanovna." He blew the whistle again. "The rest of you . . . resume War!"

15

LAIKA

AFTER WHAT FELT LIKE A lifetime in the box with nothing but the darkness and her own thoughts, Laika couldn't quite believe it when the door to the Black Eternity finally opened.

Sunlight poured in. Laika shakily pushed herself up to all fours, her limbs aching from the cramped space. She blinked hard, overcome with sounds and smells. Whiskers was there, and Soft Hands, and the Hairless Leader. Soft Hands removed the harness from her rump and they poked and prodded her with a variety of pointy sticks, nodding in satisfaction, and then Whiskers called out to someone.

The stable door rolled back to reveal another person. It was Good Girl!

As soon as Soft Hands set Laika on the floor, she raced to Good Girl. She barked, spinning in a circle around

Good Girl's feet. Her jaw hung open, her tongue lolling out and her eyes bright.

Good Girl swept her up in her arms, squeezing her so tightly that for a moment Laika couldn't breathe, before Good Girl gave her a kiss on her nose. She clipped a leash to Laika's collar and they walked together into the bright sunlight of the courtyard.

After countless days in the Black Eternity, Laika was overwhelmed with the new smells coming from the grass and sidewalks. She sniffed through the snow, savoring each scent and the information it told her about the birds who had landed here, the mouse who had run there, the oil brought in on a soldier's boots. She was so excited to be out of the box that it wasn't until Good Girl made a small, sad sound that Laika stopped. Her ears went up.

Good Girl was wiping at her face with her mitten. Her eyes were wet. She was crying, but not like Mushka did, with piteous wails. She wrapped her arms around herself like she was cold, and Laika suddenly remembered how hard Good Girl had squeezed her, as though she'd needed a friend very badly. Why? What was wrong?

She ran to Good Girl's side with a questioning bark. *Are you okay?*

Good Girl sank onto one of the benches. Laika jumped up next to her. It was then that Laika noticed a scratch on Good Girl's cheek. It was fresh, though no longer bleeding.

Her fur bristled. *Did someone hurt Good Girl?* She

sniffed and picked up the scent of other children. Boy children. Their scent was sour.

A rumble of movement at the other side of the courtyard stole her attention. Her ears pricked up. The gate was moving. Two soldiers pushed it open for a military truck waiting on the other side, black smoke coughing from its underside. The soldiers weren't paying attention to the girl and the dog.

Laika's spine went rigid as she remembered how badly she had once longed for this moment. An open gate. A chance to escape. She had even earned the people's trust, learned how to slip the collar and leash. There'd been a time when she'd been desperate for that open road beyond the gate, the forest, the city somewhere beyond.

It's not too late, a small voice whispered in her head. *You can still run.*

Her whole life, she had lived by a simple code: *The only way to survive is alone.* But as she watched the soldiers waving the truck through the gate, she realized that those were the beliefs of a desperate dog. One who had never known the warm lap of a girl.

The soldiers rolled the gate shut and locked it with a thud. Laika flinched.

Good Girl let out another quiet sob.

Laika turned back to her. *This* was where she was meant to be. She didn't know if people and dogs could be part of the same pack, and she didn't care. Good Girl *was* part of her pack. There was something missing in Good Girl in the same way there had always been something missing in Laika. She'd thought only dogs could be Cold—struggling to trust others, guarding their hearts against the world—but if she was certain of anything, it was that Good Girl was Cold, too. Maybe Albina had gotten the story wrong. Maybe Laika hadn't met Good Girl so that she could one day become a Warm Dog. Maybe it was so that *Laika* could help *Good Girl* become a Warm Girl.

Laika smelled her all over. The scratch on her cheek. The tears in her eyes. The snow on her coat. The reek of boys who'd meant ill, just like the dog pack that had attacked Laika. Her mind suddenly filled with understanding: *A pack of children had attacked Good Girl.*

She felt a growl rise deep within her. It was like she was back in the shoe-store alley, scrappy and hungry and ready to defend herself at any costs. Except now it was Good Girl she would fight for.

The Dog Star was right, she thought. *Some people are cruel, just as some people are kind.*

Laika rested her paws on Good Girl's shoulder and licked the tears off her face. Good Girl squirmed like it tickled, and a hint of a smile touched her lips.

A boy's voice cut across the courtyard. Suddenly Good Girl's smile disappeared.

Laika spun around, growling low. It was Good Girl's young brother. The thin, red-cheeked one. He was calling to his sister.

Laika sniffed the air.

Sour.

The boy was one of Good Girl's attackers! Her own brother! Laika's hackles rose as another growl rumbled up her throat. She jumped off Good Girl's lap and lunged at him.

The boy screamed and ran.

Laika gave a toothy, satisfied smile. She hadn't drawn blood—she'd only torn his pants as a warning. *I won't let anyone hurt my pack*, she thought.

She trotted back to Good Girl with her tail held high.

Good Girl wiped away the last of her tears. She swept Laika into her arms. "Good girl, Laika. Good girl!"

Laika's tail wagged happily back and forth.

16

NINA

"GO WASH UP, BOTH OF you," Mama instructed as soon as they got home. "We have guests for supper. Your father's colleagues." She pinched the skin at her throat anxiously. Ivan ran upstairs, but as Nina passed by, Mama stopped her.

"The scratch on your cheek," she said quietly. "Did this happen at school?"

Nina flinched as she thought of the snowballs assaulting her, even Ivan's. But how could she tell Mama that they had called her a traitor, when Mama had hammered into her how important it was to distance herself from Ludmilla?

"An icicle fell from the school roof," Nina muttered without looking up and went upstairs. The lie sat uneasy with her. Lies and secrets were everywhere—not even she could escape telling them.

By the time the doorbell rang, Nina had brushed her hair and pinned it with a barrette, and she was wearing her red dress with the puffy sleeves, even though she hated it. There were three men with Papa. Director Sonin from the lab, and two men in suits and large black hats that, when removed, revealed similar oiled hairstyles.

"Welcome, administrators." Mama came out of the kitchen, in red lipstick and wearing a new dress under her apron. She took their coats and hats. "I'm Lidia, and these are our children, Ivan and Nina. I'm sorry, Konstantin hasn't told me your names."

The administrators exchanged a glance.

Papa cleared his throat. "These administrators run top secret programs, Lidia. Like the Chief Designer, they must remain nameless."

Mama blushed. "Of course. How foolish of me."

"Not at all!" one of the administrators bellowed. "Protocol can be onerous at times. Call me Comrade Bolshoi, and my companion Comrade Grom."

Mama hesitated at the odd nicknames. *Comrade Big* and *Comrade Thunder*. She smiled uneasily and shook their hands.

After small talk, everyone moved to the table. When Mama lifted the silver lid off the main dish, Nina grimaced. Shuba. Sometimes it was called Herring Under a Fur Coat. Mama's cooking was never particularly memorable, and this ambitious purple-colored dish—fish, potato, and beets smothered in mayonnaise and chopped egg—wasn't one of her better meals.

Papa suddenly looked very pale. "Ah, sit, please."

The administrators complimented Mama on the presentation, but after a few bites, quietly set their forks down and tried not to look green.

Comrade Grom reached for the bread basket.

Comrade Bolshoi turned to Nina and Ivan and cleared his throat. "Comrade Lidia, your children attend the grade school near Lenin Park, yes? Excellent school director there, Comrade Stepko. Highly respected in the Communist Party."

Nina must have made a face, because her mother gave her a quick kick under the table. But above the table, her mother was all smiles.

"Indeed," Mama said. "I believe Director Stepko organized a game of War today for the Young Pioneers. An excellent way to teach our Soviet youth the lessons of bravery and sacrifice. Did you enjoy the game, children?"

Nina kept her jaw clenched tightly, pushing around small mountains of shuba on her plate.

"I did," Ivan said, and after a pause added, "Nina wouldn't play. Everyone got angry with her and she had to sit out the rest of the game."

The conversation around the table died. Panic crossed her mother's face as the administrators shared a suspecting look between each other.

Nina thought fast. She set her fork down and turned to her brother with a laugh. "Ivan, it sounds wrong when you say it like that." She turned to the administrators. "I was playing on the side of the Americans. We don't choose sides—it's based on year number. Naturally I didn't want to be an American, so I refused to play . . . I can't bring myself to harm fellow Soviets, even if it's only pretend."

The worry on the administrators' faces eased. Comrade Grom slowly nodded, impressed by her fervor.

Ivan opened his mouth, but Mama quickly interrupted. "Oh, look, we're out of wine. Children, go get another bottle from the kitchen." She gave Nina a hard look.

Nina grabbed Ivan's hand and pulled him out of his seat before he could say another word. She dragged him into the kitchen, eased the door closed, and then turned to her brother and hissed, "Not another word about War."

"Mama brought it up!"

"Are you trying to get me in trouble? Get Papa arrested?"

"Of course not! Why would anyone arrest Papa? I was only answering their question. They're officials, Nina. We can't *lie* to them."

She drew in a deep breath. Her body still ached from the snowballs, but when she looked at her little brother's confused face, she sighed. She couldn't let him go on believing that the Party was more important than their own family.

Glancing at the door, she said quietly, "I'm going to tell you something and you must never repeat it. Not to your teachers, not to Director Stepko, to no one. Can I trust you?"

His eyes went wide. He paused, then nodded.

She turned on the sink faucet to muffle their words. "While we were at Papa's lab, the Chief Designer told me that Ludmilla's father didn't work with Papa and the dogs.

He did something with missiles. Missiles can carry *bombs*. Do you see? That's why everyone is so worried about his defection. They are afraid he's sharing his research with the Americans. They could declare war on us and use those missiles against us."

Ivan's eyes went wider.

Nina continued quietly, "I don't think the administrators are really here to eat Mama's food and ask us about school. I think they're trying to make sure we aren't going to defect, too. That Papa won't try to sell *his* research to the Americans."

"He would never!" Ivan gasped.

"Of course not. But let's not give them any reason to question us."

He blinked hard, frowning. "I don't understand. They don't say any of this in Young Pioneer rallies. Or on the radio. Or in school."

"Exactly. That's why we're whispering about it in the kitchen."

He looked close to tears, and Nina softened. She gave him a gentle poke in the ribs. "Everything is going to be fine. But if you get me in trouble for not playing War, I'll send the Bukavac after you."

He smiled a little as he dodged her tickle. "I—"

"*Shhh.*" Nina suddenly pressed a finger to her lips, her head cocked toward the doorway. She thought she'd heard the adults in the dining room mention something about dogs. She cracked the kitchen door.

Outside, Papa was saying, "We need more time. We haven't had a chance to fully train the dogs. And the rocket itself, well, we've rushed its construction to be ready for the New Year's celebration. Key pieces of technology remain missing. Until we develop a dependable retrieval system—"

"The Chief Designer feels very strongly about the timing," one of the administrators cut in. Judging by his voice, it was the big one, Comrade Bolshoi. "It's non-negotiable. The order comes from the premier himself. Take shortcuts if you must."

His words made the hair on the back of Nina's arms rise.

Director Sonin quickly stated, "Rest assured, Administrator Bolshoi, the rocket will be ready in time for the New Year's celebration. There will be no delays."

Papa remained silent. Nina peeked through the cracked door and read his anger in the way he clenched his fork with white knuckles.

When she and Ivan returned with a new bottle of wine, the air in the dining room felt sticky and thick, the same consistency as Mama's shuba. The wine bottle became too heavy in her hands, so she set it on the table with a thud.

For a moment, everyone was silent until Mama picked up the wine with a nervous smile. "More to drink, comrades?"

Administrator Grom held up his glass.

Director Sonin turned to Nina and Ivan with a warm smile, all hints of their tense argument gone now. "Children, perhaps you can help us settle a friendly debate.

You've met all three dogs, yes? Only one will go to space. I'm partial to Albina, since she has already flown two missions and we know she can handle difficult conditions. But your father prefers Laika. Which would you choose?"

The color had returned to Ivan's cheeks, though he looked a little wary after the conversation in the kitchen. He said slowly, "Not Albina. She's too ugly."

The adults burst out in laughter, and Nina saw her mother relax, but only just a little.

"I wouldn't call the old girl ugly," Papa said. "But it is true that she is perhaps not as . . . photogenic as the others."

"The dog's photograph will be published widely." Administrator Grom ripped into a piece of bread. "We need the world to fall in love with her. With *us*—with the Motherland. This dog represents the best of the Soviet Union. Strength, character, bravery. The dog must reflect the pleasing and healthy nature of our citizens."

"What about the fluffy one?" Director Sonin asked. "The loud one? She's good-looking."

"Mushka is charismatic," Papa agreed, "but she has trouble sitting quietly for long periods of time."

Nina felt a flutter in her chest. "Laika is very pretty," she offered. She paused, trying to think through what they would want to hear. "When I see her, I think of our comrades toiling in the fields and factories, proud and humble."

"What a poetic way to put it, Comrade Nina." Administrator Bolshoi tipped his wineglass toward her.

"Nina is very fond of the dogs," Papa explained. "She's

caring for them as part of a Young Pioneer service project. Laika is your favorite, isn't she, Nina?"

As all eyes turned to her, Nina felt suddenly like her dress was too tight. She gulped water. But then she set down her glass and announced fiercely, "I love her."

For some reason, the men burst out in laughter again. Heat rose to Nina's cheeks.

"There, you see?" Administrator Bolshoi pounded the table. "Already, the dog is beloved! You're quite right to love her, Nina Konstantinova. Soon the whole world will love her, too." He turned to Papa. "What do you say? Shall we make it official? With an endorsement like that, how can we not?"

Papa folded his hands on the table. "Laika did score the highest marks on all three tests." He glanced at Director Sonin. "It is your department. You have the final call, comrade."

Director Sonin sat back in his chair, considered this for some time, and then clapped his hands together. "Very well. Laika is our starflyer!"

Nina sat up straighter. "Laika's going to space? Really?"

Papa gave her hand a pat. "Yes, lapochka. And we'll take Albina to the cosmodrome, too, as her backup."

"When is the launch?" Ivan had perked up again. "Can we see the rocket? I bet it looks just like my model!"

"Darling, the launch site is all the way in Kazakhstan," Mama chided. "Papa will have to take an airplane."

Ivan's eyes lit up more. "I want to ride in an airplane, Papa!"

"The launch site is at a top secret location," Papa began. "I cannot imagine children would be permitted—"

Comrade Grom stopped him. His eyebrow slowly traveled upward as he studied Ivan and Nina.

"Wait, wait, comrade." He turned to the other men, tapping his finger on the table. "Images from the launch will be broadcast to every major country in the world. We've invited journalists to attend the launch for that exact reason—loyal journalists and photographers who can be trusted. Look at these children: a strong, handsome boy and girl. Children of Star City, of the Communist Party. What would look better than to have the children of Russia present at the launch, proudly wearing the red kerchiefs of the Young Pioneers, as much a symbol of our promising future as the dog itself?"

Administrator Bolshoi and Director Sonin considered this for a while, stroking their chins. Nina felt an anxious flutter in her heart. Ride in an airplane? Be photographed for newspapers? Watch Laika make history with her own two eyes?

"Papa, can we?" she whispered. "I could help take care of Laika."

He placed his big hand over hers. "That will be a very delicate time. She'll need to undergo an operation prior to the launch to insert sensors beneath her skin so we can monitor her heart rate and respiration. I'm afraid you can't be there for that."

Nina's face fell. "An operation? Will she be okay? Will you be able to take out the sensors when she returns?"

The adults remained quiet, and Nina hesitated, uncertain.

Her father squeezed Nina's hand and said softly, "Orbital technology has never been attempted before. Laika will be the first living creature in outer space. As with any new technology, there comes uncertainty."

Nina blinked. "Yes, I know, but Svetlana said that you're working to ensure Laika's safety. That she'll come back unharmed. Like Albina did."

"Albina's flights were much simpler, lapochka. She was able to come back down on a parachute."

"So use a parachute for Laika, too."

Papa tilted his head to one side, and he started to speak, but Administrator Bolshoi interjected, "Such worries, child! The dog will be fine. She'll be a hero. When those cameras take your photograph at the launch site, you must look happy and confident. All will go well!"

Her father exchanged a long look with Director Sonin.

Mama brought out a small bottle of sherry. She poured it into tiny glasses and even gave a small amount to Ivan and Nina. Nina looked into the honey-colored liquid, wishing she could talk to Ludmilla, tell her about Laika and about the launch and about War and everything else. But Boston might as well have been on a different planet.

Mama lifted her glass. "To Laika. To the dog who will chase the stars."

They all raised their glasses. "To the dog who will chase the stars!"

17

LAIKA

LAIKA AWOKE TO A FLASHING light and a sharp *pop* outside her crate.

When she lifted her eyelids, the light flashed again. *Pop!* A starburst filled her vision with dancing dots, and she stood up, disoriented. So many voices filled the parlor! Her vision began to clear and she found herself staring through her crate bars into a round silver cone with a light bulb in the middle, attached to a black box that a man in a brown coat held to his eye.

Pop!

The light went off again, but this time she knew better and squeezed her eyes shut before the flash.

"Albina, who are all these people?" she barked.

"They've come from Moscow. I smell the city on their clothes. And ink. Ah! The Ink Men! They take pictures and write stories for newspapers."

Mushka's ears swiveled backward. "When I was a Warm Dog, my family would smack my bottom with newspapers." She started shaking.

"I don't believe these men have come to smack your bottom," Albina said, then turned back to Laika. "They came when I flew before."

Laika's ears rose.

Whiskers and Soft Hands entered the parlor, along with the Hairless Leader. The leader moved with more nervous energy than usual. He clapped his hands together and spoke a few words to the Ink Men.

Laika watched as they shook his hand one at a time, big smiles on their faces.

Whiskers opened her crate. Laika had come to trust Whiskers—he was Good Girl's father, and since Good Girl was now a member of her pack, Whiskers was, too—but with all the new people in the room, her heart was pitter-pattering wildly. As he wrapped his hands around her small body, she snatched up Good Girl's blue blanket in her jaws.

Whiskers turned to the Ink Men and said something that made them laugh. He spoke a few words to Laika and gently tugged the blanket from her jaws. Laika held firm. But after a few more tugs, she relented.

"Good girl." He put the scrap of fabric in his jacket pocket.

The Hairless Leader announced something in a booming voice, and Whiskers thrust Laika up in the air. Her heart raced faster. He held her over his head, his hands sturdy on her rump and chest. Did he feel how fast her heart was beating?

When she looked over, Soft Hands was holding up Albina proudly, too.

The Ink Men tumbled over one another to click their black boxes again. Laika's vision was filled with blinding white dots. She couldn't see where Whiskers carried her next. She sniffed. Listened. Judging by the echo of their footsteps, it was the hallway that led to the courtyard. The Ink Men were coming with them.

"Albina? Are you still there? I can't see!"

"I can't, either."

Laika's vision cleared as they reached the courtyard, where a fleet of black cars waited. A driver opened the door for them.

Whiskers and Soft Hands let the two dogs loose on the seat between them. Whiskers reached into his bag and pulled out files to show to Soft Hands, who put on her glasses and nodded.

Laika jumped up on Whiskers's lap and stood on her hind legs to peer out the window. "We're leaving Star City," she reported to Albina. "Driving through the forest." She whirled around, watching the gates rumble closed, a low whine escaping her jaw. "We left Mushka behind!"

Albina jumped into Soft Hands's lap and looked out the opposite window. For as much as the old dog complained about Mushka's incessant yips, she let out a worried whine, too.

The black car rolled through the forest. There were clumps of snow beneath the trees, bleeding into brown mud. Birds fluttered from branch to branch. The sun was low and hazy. The car went over a bump, and one of Whiskers's files bounced open. A piece of paper fell onto the car floor.

"Laika, look!" Albina barked.

It was a poster of a dog with a white body, chocolate-brown face, and perky ears. The dog peered valiantly toward the sky. A capsule like the one in the training rooms in Star City rested below the dog. Stars danced in the sky in the background.

"That's you!" Albina exclaimed.

Laika jumped down from the window, cocking her head at the drawing. "Is it really?" Other than her reflection in shop windows, she'd never seen an image of herself. Was that what she looked like? Big dark eyes? Chin tipped up proudly?

She wagged her tail.

Albina stood on all fours, her nails pattering excitedly on the seat. "That's a rocket ship below you, Laika. You're going to space!"

Laika lifted her ears.

I'm going to fly?

But just as soon as a prickle of excitement ruffled her fur, she straightened. "I can't fly yet! I haven't said goodbye to Good Girl. I have to promise that I'll come back."

Albina rested a reassuring paw on her shoulder. "I

haven't seen any starflyer suits. I don't believe today is for flying. I think today is only for taking photographs and writing about you so that everyone will know about the brave thing you will do."

Laika's breath slowed in relief. She sat down, feeling the comforting rhythm of the moving car. "If I'm going to space, why did they bring you, too?"

"They probably knew you would need a friend."

Laika panted happily. "Yes, and they were right. I'm glad I'm not alone."

They rode in silence the rest of the trip. Laika stared out the car window at the sky. Was it true that one day soon she would be *up* there? Above the clouds? Even higher than the birds? And Good Girl would be here, waiting for Laika to return so she could make her a Warm Dog forever.

The car pulled into another gated facility and parked. Laika jumped onto Whiskers's lap to look out the window again. They were back in the city! She recognized the tall steel tower near the river, the one that she'd always used as a landmark to orient herself around the blocks surrounding the shoe store.

As soon as the people in white coats carried them inside, Laika was assaulted with hundreds of smells. New people, new animals, new foods. They went into a box the size of a closet, which suddenly started moving upward. When the box stopped and the doors opened, the flashing pops began again.

More Ink Men were here—dozens of them!

Whiskers rested a hand on Laika's back, murmuring reassuring words.

The Hairless Leader swept over with several men in big hats. The Big Hats shook hands with Whiskers and Soft Hands as the room filled with excited chatter. Now Laika's heart raced for a different reason. They were here for *her*! They wanted to see her, to take pictures of her, to pat her on the head. No one had shoes in their hands to throw at her. People were lining up to tell her what a good girl she was.

The Hairless Leader picked her up. Her muscles tensed as he carried her to a desk that held a piece of machinery that looked like a metal ice cream cone.

The Ink Men took more pictures. *Pop pop pop!*

The Hairless Leader leaned forward to speak into the metal ice cream cone. The Ink Men wrote furiously in their notebooks. *Scratch scratch scratch.* Albina watched from far in the back, cradled by Soft Hands.

Suddenly the room went quiet. The Hairless Leader had stopped speaking. With a dizzying sense, Laika realized that everyone was looking at her. Dozens of eyes were eagerly awaiting . . . something. What? What did they want? Their little wooden sticks hovered above paper. Their fingers waited to press the buttons of their black boxes.

Her heart pounded. What did they want her to do?

Whiskers tapped the metal ice cream cone and looked at her expectantly, then said a word she knew from her days in the streets, a word the cobbler's wife used to yell at her to stop doing.

"Bark," Whiskers said.

Laika knew she must do as they wished, so she leaned close to the metal ice cream cone. The Ink Men leaned in, too.

She barked once, short and high.

The room erupted in applause. Dozens of flashing lights went off. Laika stood a little bit taller. She tilted her chin up like in the poster.

By the time they had finished taking photographs, the sun was sinking low. Laika's belly began to rumble, reminding her of the supper that would be waiting for her in her crate. When Whiskers put her in the car's back seat, she looked dreamily up at the stars.

The Dog Star shone down on her, pulsing gently.

Good girl, Laika.

But instead of climbing into the back with her, Whiskers got into the driver's seat, started the car, and drove deeper into Moscow. Laika lifted her ears in surprise. Where were they going if not back to Star City? Where was Soft Hands? And Albina? They'd brought Albina all the way to Moscow so Laika would have a friend, so why leave her behind now? But when she met Whiskers's eyes in the rearview mirror, a soft smile touched his lips.

He winked.

18

NINA

NINA FIXED HER ATTENTION ON the radio set in the living room. She'd gathered with Mama and Ivan to hear Laika's famous bark, the one newspapers said would be "heard around the world." After the broadcast, Mama went to the kitchen to finish cooking supper, while Nina kept adjusting the dial. "*The great Soviet Union is working to bring near the time when human travel in space will be a reality,*" a scientist said, "*when people in spaceships will be able to establish contact with other distant, hitherto unknown worlds. No other nation even comes close to rivaling our technology . . .*"

Ivan leaned close to Nina and whispered, "When the administrators were here, you said in the kitchen that we can't trust what people say on the radio. So how do we know if the Soviet Union is really the greatest?"

Nina hesitated. It hadn't been long ago that she had

believed everything she heard on the radio and in school, too. But all that had changed since she'd learned that Ludmilla's family had left out of fear for their lives. There was a lot about their country that they weren't taught in school.

"Well, *some* of what they say is true," she said slowly. "But sometimes leaders believe that it's okay to lie if their intentions are good. It isn't easy to sort out truth from lies, and there's a whole ocean of half-truths in between." She squeezed his shoulder. "Listen to your heart. And to Mama and Papa. That's how you'll know what to believe."

"Director Stepko says our loyalty must be to the Party, not our families."

"Director Stepko can go sit on a tack," she scoffed. "He doesn't make you solyanka soup when you're sick, or take you sledding in the park, or spend all day helping you paint model rockets, does he?"

A car horn sounded outside the town house.

"It's Papa!" Ivan jumped up and ran to the door.

Nina kept her attention on the radio, hoping for more details. She didn't want to miss a word about Laika's mission. Static wavered as she adjusted the knob.

She heard the front door open and Papa's voice, but she kept trying to get a clear station.

Then another sound came from the doorway.

"Bark!"

At first she thought she'd heard it on the radio. But then little nails clicked on the hardwood floor and she turned with a gasp as a ball of fur thundered onto her lap.

She blinked in surprise.

"Laika?"

The dog licked her face.

She looked up at her father in wonder. "Papa . . . but how?"

"In a few days Laika will travel to the cosmodrome. I wanted to do something nice for her first. One night to have a home away from the Institute. To just be a dog: to bark and play." He knelt down, scratching Laika behind the ears. "Can you do that for her, lapochka?"

Nina nodded solemnly. "I will, Papa."

Papa stood up and patted Ivan on the shoulder. "You as well, Ivan. Give Laika a good memory to take with her in the rocket, yes?"

Ivan nodded.

Their father loosened his tie as he went upstairs. From the sounds in the kitchen, Mama was chopping vegetables for solyanka soup.

Ivan knelt cautiously next to Laika.

"Afraid she'll bite your pants again?" Nina asked.

He looked down sheepishly. "A little."

"Here. We'll play fetch with her." Nina's eyes settled on an object by the front door. "Pick that up, Ivan."

Ivan picked up the scrap of blue fabric and then asked in surprise as he handed it to her, "Is this part of Ludmilla's old scarf?"

"Yes. I gave it to Laika. I couldn't bear to toss it out."

The fabric was badly chewed but well loved. Nina ran her fingers over the familiar silky wool, then tied it into a thick knot. She tossed it across the room. "Come on, Laika. Fetch!"

Laika tumbled across the rug after the ball of wool as though she'd been playing fetch all her life. She snatched it in her teeth, shook it, and then trotted back proudly to Nina, who laughed and scratched her head. "What a good girl! Your turn, Ivan."

Nina tossed him the toy. Ivan, grinning, threw it farther, so far that it flew into the kitchen and Laika scrambled after it. They heard a startled shriek from their mother and then a banging of pots and pans. Laika's nails scrabbled on the kitchen floor.

Nina and Ivan jumped up. Nina's heart was racing. *Mama might scold us, might send Laika back . . .*

But an unexpected sound rolled out of the kitchen.

Mama started laughing!

Ivan and Nina exchanged a surprised look. They ran to the kitchen and stopped short in the doorway. Soup was splattered everywhere: on the counter, on the stove, on the walls, even on Mama's cheek. A puddle covered the floor by Mama's feet, and in the middle of the puddle Laika was licking up broth as fast as her tongue could move.

Their mother looked up. Her face was pink, her eyes bright. She looked beautiful, even splattered in soup. "That tattered old scarf came flying in the doorway and landed right in the soup pot! And wouldn't you know, Laika came leaping up right after! I was so startled that I knocked over the pot and soup went everywhere."

"Oh," Nina said. Normally, this would have made Mama anxious. "And that's . . . okay?"

Mama waved away the worry. "It's only solyanka soup. We'll have something else for dinner. Cheese and bread." She grinned and knelt down to pet Laika. "Wouldn't you like that, little one? Cheese and bread?"

Nina stared at her mother as though she was a creature from another planet that had stolen a ride back to Earth on one of Papa's rockets. "You aren't mad that I kept Ludmilla's scarf without telling you? That I gave it to Laika and . . . she ruined your soup?"

"Darling, look at Laika. How happy she is. At least *someone* likes my cooking."

It was true, Laika was still licking up the beef broth as though she'd never tasted anything as scrumptious. She gazed up at them, her eyes softened, jaw open and relaxed.

"No one would recognize Ludmilla's scarf now," Mama said, brushing the spot of soup off her cheek. "I don't see the harm in letting the dog keep the thing. Why don't you take her to play in the back alley? I'll make us a light dinner and call you when it's ready."

Nina wasn't about to argue. She and Ivan put on coats and took Laika to the fenced-in alleyway at the rear of the building. It was where Mama threw out the laundry water and, in the summertime, set out pots for growing carrots, though there was rarely enough sun to make them grow longer than Nina's thumb.

Nina and Ivan played fetch with Laika, and then, when the cold got too much, they brought her inside and dressed her up in Nina's old baby clothes from the attic, laughing as she paraded around in tiny dresses and bonnets. When their mother set supper on the table—apple slices, a hunk of cheese, fresh bread from the bakery, and some cold chicken from the night before—their father came down and joined them. He pulled out a seat for Laika at the head of the table, calling her the Hero of Moscow.

After supper, Nina cradled Laika in her arms up the stairs to her bedroom. Her desk lamp was on. She sat on the floor with Laika in her lap and opened a book. Laika had seemed to enjoy the pictures in "The Firebird and the Gray Wolf," so she read from her collection of folk tales until she was yawning and Laika's eyes were closing.

Ivan appeared in the doorway and Nina jumped, half asleep.

"Ivan? Is everything all right?" she asked.

He came in and sat across from them. He took a deep breath. "I've been thinking about what you said and . . . I'm sorry about the snowball."

She bristled at the memory, but then softened. She thought of how, when they were younger, she used to hear Ivan crying during nightmares and would sleep on the floor of his room to protect him from bad dreams.

"It's okay, little monster. But from now on, we listen

to each other before any teachers or administrators, okay? And no more snowballs . . . unless they're aimed at Pyotr."

He grinned. Together, they watched snow falling on rooftops beyond her window. Nina thought about Laika out there on the streets, in the cold. She hugged the sleepy little dog harder.

Laika had a family now. A family that nothing could break.

19

LAIKA

LAIKA HADN'T FALLEN ASLEEP quite yet.

Had there ever been a more perfect day? Memories chased one another through her mind as she dozed in Good Girl's arms: fetching the blanket, licking soup off the floor, eating cheese from a real china plate, and most of all, Good Girl. Good Girl holding her. Good Girl kissing her. Good Girl stroking the hairs on her nose. Laika hadn't even minded when her brother joined them for a while, but she was still glad when he left and she had Good Girl to herself.

Good Girl yawned and rubbed the sleep out of her eyes. She crawled into bed, patting the covers, and Laika jumped up to join her. Good Girl hugged her to her chest. She didn't say a word, just held Laika in the warmth of her arms.

Soon Good Girl's breathing grew deeper as she sank

into sleep. Laika rested her head against Good Girl's shoulder. The stars twinkled beyond the window.

Laika searched the sky for the brightest one and said quietly, "I have a girl. I have a warm bed. I have food. Am I a Warm Dog now?"

Not quite, the Dog Star answered.

"I mastered the three tricks, didn't I?"

You did. But there is one final thing the people will ask of you.

Laika shook her head. "I don't want to return to the laboratory. Good Girl's been Cold for a long time . . . She's finally getting Warm. She needs me."

The light of the Dog Star gleamed brighter. *The world needs you, too. That is why they have chosen you. You inspire them. Do you see how, just with your presence, you have brought this family together? Soon you will bring together the whole world. All people dream of the stars. You are the symbol of that dream.*

Laika's stomach twisted. "Albina says this mission is even more dangerous than facing a pack of dogs in the alley." Her paws began to tremble. She still bore the scars of her fight with the dog pack. She'd feared for her life then. How much more danger could she take? How far could a little dog's bravery go?

The warm light shone down on her.

Would you go back, if you could? Do you still think of escape?

Laika looked up at Good Girl's sleeping face. Her lips

were pursed like a doll's. Her brown curls tangled around one another. Even if she had wanted to return to the shoe-store stoop, it was impossible now. Her heart was here with this messy-haired girl.

She cuddled closer to Good Girl.

"Where would I escape to?" she told the Dog Star. "I'm already home."

20

NINA

DESPITE THE PALE BLUE SKIES, it was another cold day in Moscow. Nina and the rest of her year stood in the school courtyard, blowing into their mittened hands and shaking some warmth into their legs as they waited for Director Stepko to speak. It had been three days since the night Laika had come to their house, and Nina missed the dog fiercely. Papa and the other scientists had packed their bags and moved into Star City, where they were spending every day and every night prepping Laika and Albina—as her backup—for the launch. Nina checked the clock on the schoolhouse tower. In just a few hours, Papa and Laika and the others would leave on an airplane for Baikonur Cosmodrome in Kazakhstan. And the day after tomorrow, before the sun rose, Nina would join them, along with Mama and Ivan.

"Can't we all travel together?" Nina had asked Papa before he left for Star City.

"No, lapochka. You'll see her at the cosmodrome in a few days, I promise."

Nina was worried about Laika, but beneath the fear was a flutter of excitement. They were going to ride in a real airplane! She would see all of Moscow from high above, though not as high as Laika would be in the rocket, of course. She'd cheer as Laika's capsule rose to the sky and the whole world watched the dog's journey.

Suddenly the school's bugle boy blasted his instrument, horribly off-key.

"Thank you," Director Stepko said, tugging at one ear as he stepped onto the dais. "Today we have a surprise in honor of the upcoming launch of Sputnik II, with the brave Soviet dog Laika on board."

Nina was happy to hear Laika's name but not surprised. Her name was on everyone's lips, from the mail carrier to the reporters on the radio.

The director continued, "Comrade Gammel from the state's animal control department has come to lead us on a field trip to demonstrate how we may be good citizens to our canine comrades. The true test of any nation is not how they treat their most prominent neighbors, but their humblest."

A ripple of excitement warmed the shivering students. Spending time with dogs made for a much better afternoon than memorizing multiplication tables.

Tatyanna leaned over to Nina. "Better than War, eh?"

Nina was so excited about the launch that not even the memory of that awful game troubled her.

Director Stepko turned to a thin man wearing the forest-green jumpsuit of animal control. "Comrade Gammel, would you like to explain today's field trip?"

The dogcatcher removed his hat and stepped awkwardly onto the dais, looking like he was more at home with four-legged creatures than children. "You'll see that on this table to the right, your teachers have wrapped today's lunch scraps in newspaper bundles. Each student may take a bundle. We will walk in pairs through the park and nearby streets to feed the neighborhood's stray dogs."

Director Stepko chimed in. "By contributing food scraps to our city's dogs, we are spreading the values of our great Communist Party: sharing resources, reducing wasteful practices, and supporting all members of society. We Soviets do not overlook our less fortunate; we are a nation where even stray dogs are given respect, even given the opportunity to rise to the stars. Now pair up and take a packet of scraps."

Tatyanna and Nina approached the table and took greasy packets wrapped in newspaper. Nina unwrapped a corner and peeked inside. Fish heads and tails from the cod served at lunch, along with some bread crusts soaked in milk.

They followed Gammel and their teacher escorts toward the river, where the dogcatcher explained that many dogs sheltered around the bridges, sniffing out rubbish or dead fish.

Nina thought of the sad wooden crate that Laika had called home in the shoe-store alley. Despite Director Stepko's insistence that strays lived a noble life, she felt deeply relieved that Laika would never return there.

"When do you leave?" Tatyanna asked excitedly.

"Day after tomorrow, before dawn."

"Won't you be frightened to fly on an airplane?" Tatyanna asked.

Nina shook her head. "Oh, no. I want to see the world from up high. Besides, it's the only way to get to the cosmodrome, and I want to give Laika a kiss for good luck before her launch."

Tatyanna sighed. "I wish I could go with you!"

A pair of their classmates, the twins Borya and Maks, stopped ahead to give their scraps to a shaggy old gray dog curled up beneath a bench, who wagged her tail happily. As soon as the smell of fish spread through the air, a few more shy dogs poked their noses out from under scraggly bushes and mailboxes. Somehow, word spread through the dog world, and soon there were a dozen strays wagging their tails, surrounding the class.

The students giggled and tossed scraps to the excited dogs.

"Look, Nina, that one looks a little like Laika, don't you think?" Tatyanna pointed to a small brown-and-white mutt sheltering under an apartment building's stairs, her nose raised and sniffing the air. Nina and Tatyanna called to her until she padded forward shyly.

"This is for you, comrade dog," Tatyanna said and tossed a piece of bread. Nina knelt down and held out another piece, calling softly.

"Here, girl. Food for you on a cold day. Come on, don't be shy. The dogcatcher hasn't come for you today."

"Try offering the fish," Borya said.

When Nina held out a piece of fish, the little dog crept forward and devoured it anxiously.

"Excellent, students," Director Stepko said. "These dogs might not fly on a rocket like Laika, but they keep our streets clean of scraps and they kill the rats that would make us ill. They are valuable workers."

Nina scratched the little dog under the chin. "It might be a noble job to catch mice, but a difficult one just the same. I wish I could take you all to Star City. Don't you want to fly to the stars?"

Borya, who had overheard, drew in a sharp breath. Maks shushed him loudly. They shared a look between each another.

Nina looked up at them with a frown. "What is it?"

"Nothing," Maks said, but Borya shifted from one foot to another, looking at the dogs, and mumbled sadly, "It's better for dogs on the streets. Here, at least, they have a chance."

Nina scrunched up her nose. "What do you mean? A chance to starve? Starflyer dogs have a warm place to live and good food to eat. They're famous and on the radio and everything."

Again, the twins shared a doubting look.

Nina rested her hands on her hips. "What are you two being so secretive about? I know as much as anyone about the dogs. I work with them every week alongside my father and the other scientists."

Borya glanced at his brother and then said reluctantly, "Our uncle Leo is a managing editor at *Pravda* newspaper. He often has meetings with government officials, who tell him what to publish articles about." He scratched his ear awkwardly. "And what to *leave out*."

Nina frowned. "What do you mean?"

Maks asked in a low voice, "Haven't you noticed that the newspaper stories provide many details about Laika's launch but none about her return?"

A hollow feeling filled Nina's chest. She didn't like what the twins were suggesting.

"Maybe it is classified information," Tatyanna offered.

Maks drew in a breath. "I don't think so. Uncle Leo says we do not have the technology to bring Laika back to Earth. We are sending her into space to die. He heard it from the administrators directly. They ordered him not to print that part of the story, despite rumors he had heard."

Nina leaned forward, feeling like she was about to topple over. Her vision went black.

Tatyanna grabbed her arm. "Nina, are you all right?"

She blinked through the black dots in her eyes, shaking

her head forcefully at the twins. "No, your uncle is wrong. They brought Albina back. They brought Tsygan back." She paused before admitting, "I know there have been accidents, but there is always a plan to return the dogs to Earth. My father and Svetlana Popovich wouldn't lie to me about that."

Borya said quietly, "Uncle Leo says that no one has to lie, as long as no one asks."

"I *did* ask." Nina's face was growing hot. Hadn't the subject come up at dinner with the administrators? She clearly remembered them saying Laika would be fine.

But then again, Administrator Bolshoi had said that, not Papa . . .

And while Papa didn't lie, she didn't trust the administrator to be honest.

A terrible fear filled her.

It was true that none of the newspaper articles she'd cut out and pasted on her bedroom wall explained how Laika would be returned to Earth. There were blueprints and diagrams of how the rocket would take off, but nothing about return parachutes or reentry equipment or even any mention of how long Laika would be in space.

She had told Ivan not to believe everything he heard . . . Was she guilty of doing the same?

Nina spotted her teacher and ran over. "Olenka Ivanovna, they wouldn't send Laika into space without a way to bring her back, would they? Surely you have heard a plan . . . or read about it in newspapers?"

Olenka Ivanovna looked down in consternation. "Nina Konstantinova, what are you going on about? I told you that I expected no more disruptions of this sort." But when she saw the worried look on Nina's face, she softened. "Ah. Of course you are worried about the rocket dog. We all hope for her safety. But we are not sentimental like the Americans. The work your father and his colleagues are doing will make the Soviet Union the unrivaled leader in science. They cannot send a human into space without knowing how it will affect a living creature. We must not question our officials' actions. I do not know if there is a plan for the dog's return, but regardless, sacrifices must be made. In the end, what matters is what we learn from the dog's mission, whether she survives or not."

Nina's jaw fell open. She sputtered, "It isn't right for you to say it doesn't matter if she survives! It matters to me. *She* matters to me."

Murmurs raced through the crowd as the other students overheard Nina yelling. Director Stepko caught wind and came over in a few strides. "Nina Konstantinova, quiet down at once."

"I won't!" There were tears in her eyes now, but she brushed them away. "Isn't this field trip supposed to give us respect for the common dog? Well, let me tell you about a common dog. Laika is a hero, just like all the newspapers say, but she is so much more than that. How many of you would take the risk to go to space? Who here is brave enough? She is a dog from the streets. A survivor. She likes cheese and she likes the story of 'The Firebird and the Gray Wolf.' She snores in her sleep. She's the only one who likes my mother's solyanka soup. If we respected her, we would do everything we could to bring her back."

A few students snickered, but most were silent, listening.

The teachers and Comrade Gammel the dogcatcher blinked, taken aback.

"Nina's right," Tatyanna said quietly.

Nina felt pride rising in her chest.

"Yes, why won't they tell us what will happen to the dog?" Borya piped up. "Why can't we know the truth?"

His brother nodded his agreement, and the other students began to murmur questions, too.

Director Stepko shook his head, silencing them. "Nina, return to school at once. Wait in my office until the end of the school day."

Nina folded her arms tightly as Olenka Ivanovna led her back to school. So many questions buzzed in her head. Their teachers taught them to respect even street dogs but didn't respect the students enough to tell them the truth. Maybe Ludmilla's family had left because they didn't feel safe in a country where information was so often kept secret.

Now, like Ludmilla, would Laika disappear forever, too?

21

LAIKA

IT WAS BEFORE DAWN WHEN the people in white coats came.

Mushka yawned, stretching out her limbs. "So early? They better have brought good treats."

Laika raised her tail, waiting patiently. But when Whiskers came to take her, he wasn't smiling. She lowered her tail, uncertain. Didn't he remember that magical evening, not long ago, at their home? The soup on the floor? The laughter?

She felt even more uncertain as the people in white coats took her out of her crate and strapped her down to a metal table on wheels. Laika's heart started to pound. She twisted to face Albina. "What are they doing?"

"Preparing you to fly. They did it to me when I flew, too. Cut open my skin and put wires inside. They will remove them when you return."

"So this is real now," Laika said. "Not like the Shake-Shake Box. Not the like Spinning Storm. Not like the Black Eternity."

"I think the time for tricks is over," Albina agreed.

Whiskers and Soft Hands rolled the wheeled table into a different room that she'd never seen before, with a blinding light as bright as the sun.

Laika shifted against the uncomfortable straps. She didn't like the stern lines in Whiskers's face. He took out a sharp-looking tool and, resting a hand on her back, poked her in the rump. She yelped. It was the bee sting again.

Something strange began to happen to her body. She couldn't feel her back legs. At the same time, her head felt cloudy. She lowered her head to the table—it was suddenly too heavy to keep upright.

The light was so painfully bright, her head so cloudy from the bee sting, that everything seemed to be dancing. Whiskers held a small knife. The light was aimed at her. Through it all, there was no pain. Just a tugging feeling at her body.

Soft Hands stood at her side throughout and never stopped stroking her paw.

When they finally took her back to the parlor, Mushka stopped mid-bite with goo on her snout and mumbled around her mouthful, "Laika, you look funny! There are wires and blinking things coming out of your body!"

Laika whined as the feeling began to return to her legs. "It hurts."

Albina said, "Be strong. Think of all the treats you'll get when you're finally a Warm Dog."

Whiskers set out two small crates. They were made of smooth metal and had no wire grate to look out from, only a few small air holes. Whiskers carefully lifted Laika, her heartbeat fast against his hands, and set her into the smaller crate. A chill in her bones warned her something new was about to happen. A voice inside her whispered that she might not return to Star City for a very long time.

Through the air holes, she saw them place Albina in the other crate, and Laika panted in relief. At least she wouldn't be alone.

"Be good until I see you again, Mushka," Laika barked. "Don't give the people any reason to put you back on the streets."

"Don't worry about me!"

The crate jostled as Whiskers picked it up. She heard his heavy footsteps clomping but could see only a dark hallway through the small air holes.

"Albina?" she called.

"I am here," Albina barked from the other crate. "They're bringing me, too, so you won't get lonely. So you'll have a friend."

"I'm not sure I want to fly anymore, Albina."

The older dog was quiet as they were carried down the hallway. Then she said urgently in a voice Laika hadn't heard before, "You love Good Girl, don't you?"

"With my whole heart."

"Then listen closely. I've seen a lot in my years. I haven't told you everything because some dogs don't do well with the truth." She didn't say Mushka's name, but Laika knew that the fluffy dog preferred stories with happy endings. "This is very important for you to hear. Bad things happen when missions do not go as the people in white coats plan. Years ago, there was a dog named Bobik. He didn't like it here, didn't trust the people. One day he escaped in the courtyard while a young man, Cheese Breath, was walking him."

"A dog escaped?" Laika remembered her own early plans.

"Yes, and the administrators—the men who wear big hats—were very angry with the people in white coats. This was before Whiskers and Soft Hands's time. Soldiers came and took Cheese Breath away. He was screaming and fighting against them, struggling to get free. No one ever saw him again. Several dogs believed that he was thrown into a pound for humans. A place where people are sent and never get out, never see their families again. Do you understand what I'm telling you?"

Laika flattened her ears. "You think they'll put Whiskers in . . . in something like the pound if my mission fails? But Good Girl needs her father!" Whiskers was Good Girl's protector, the leader of their human pack. Without him, how would they eat? How would they defend their home?

"I know, my friend. I know."

Laika went silent at this, considering. She hadn't realized how much was riding on her success. This was bigger than a shot at becoming a Warm Dog. Being a Warm Dog would mean nothing if Good Girl's family lost their leader.

Now she, too, would have to be a very good girl. The best girl she could possibly be.

Her thoughts vanished as they exited the hall and frigid wind blew through the crate's air holes. As the feeling slowly returned to her body, she felt herself loaded into a truck, the movement jostling the place where the people in white coats had cut into her. A sharp pain, followed by a dull ache, made her moan. An engine roared. She smelled Albina close by, and that was a comfort. She squeezed her eyes closed against the pain in her side and imagined Good Girl's arms around her.

After what felt like ages, the truck stopped. Whiskers's and Soft Hands's scents hovered nearby. The sun was rising. Through the air holes, she saw a long, empty road. There was a giant machine like a city bus with a row of round windows, but instead of four wheels it had metal wings stretched out like a bird.

A pack of Big Hats were clustered by the enormous flying machine. They said a few words to Whiskers, who answered with a nod.

Laika felt herself loaded into the flying vehicle. She pressed her eye to the air holes. They were in a narrow row of seats. The Big Hats were seated at the front of the flying machine, along with several soldiers. In the rear of the machine, Whiskers sat holding her crate, and Soft Hands sat holding Albina's.

Before she knew it, the flying machine began to rumble forward and then left the ground entirely.

22

NINA

A BRIGHT CAMERA BULB FLASHED in Nina's eyes.

She stood in front of her home with Ivan and her mother. It was so early in the morning that she was still yawning. The sun had not yet risen, and the city was shrouded in dark. She shifted in the stiff new shoes and blue coat her mother had brought for her to wear for the press conference they were scheduled to give before leaving for Laika's launch. It had been two days since the field trip when Borya and Maks had insisted that their uncle at *Pravda* said Laika wasn't coming back. Worries had been running through her mind ever since. If she could only have asked Papa, she would have answers. But he had left for Kazakhstan the day before. She wouldn't be able to ask him about it until they were at the cosmodrome.

"And you, Nina? What do you think of going to see the launch?"

She blinked, jarred. A reporter held a microphone in her direction, but he was jostled by the dozen other reporters pressing in to catch her response.

Mama reached down to adjust Nina's Young Pioneer kerchief and whispered in her ear, "Make sure this is showing for the pictures."

Nina met Mama's eyes. She'd asked Mama if the twins' uncle could be right, but Mama had been as in the dark about the truth as she had. Now, at the reporter's question, Mama gave her an expectant look. Her family had received a list of approved questions and answers the night before to study—most of them about their devotion to the Motherland, their unwavering loyalty, their pride in their father's work. Mama had helped them memorize each line, but now Nina's mind was blank.

"We are all so proud of Konstantin and his comrades at the Institute of Space Medicine," Mama said loudly, filling in Nina's line at her silence. "My daughter has even been volunteering with the dogs as part of a service project. We all help how we can. Isn't that right, Nina?" She nudged her daughter gently.

Nina nodded too hard, like her head wasn't quite attached.

"Tell us about Laika, Nina," the reporter prompted.

Nina felt her cheeks burning. Mama started to answer

for her again, but she shook her head and leaned toward the microphone, blurting out, "Laika is the bravest dog in the world. I want everyone to love her as I love her."

There were some good-natured cheers from the reporters and lots more camera bulbs flashing.

"Tell us what she was like during training."

Nina took a few quick breaths. The answers she'd been made to memorize about how Laika was cooperative in the lab felt like only part of the story. She shook her head. "Um . . . wait and watch. You will see for yourselves how special she is."

The reporters rushed to write down her words.

More cameras flashed in the predawn dark, and they asked Mama about her former work as a secretary for the Institute of Space Medicine, and Ivan about his hobby of painting model rockets. Nina couldn't shake that hollow feeling. She *had* to ask Papa if it was true about Laika not coming back. Ludmilla had left and never come back, and it had carved out a hole in Nina's heart, mended, stitch by stitch, by a little dog. How would she manage if Laika never came back, either?

Then suddenly Mama was thanking the reporters and herding Nina and Ivan toward a waiting car. It didn't take long to drive to the military runway, where a small plane waited. As dawn broke, Nina's legs felt shaky as she boarded the airplane. She thought of the headlines that might run in the newspaper the following day.

YOUNG PIONEERS FLY TO THE COSMODROME TO WISH LAIKA WELL

CHILDREN TO REPRESENT COMMUNIST YOUTH AT THE LAUNCH

GIRL SAYS GOODBYE TO DOG

She was still shaking as she took her seat on the tiny airplane next to Ivan. Across from them, Mama was crammed in with their stack of suitcases. The airplane engine started with a rumble, and Nina gasped and grabbed the edge of the seat.

"There's no reason to worry," Mama said. "The administrators assure me that air travel is perfectly safe." But Mama was clutching her seat, too. She muttered under her breath to herself, "And they would *never* lie."

The airplane began to roll down the runway. Through a window to the cockpit, Nina watched the back of the two pilots' heads. The airplane raced faster, and with a jolt, rose. The sound of wheels on the runway vanished. Ivan grabbed her hand. Nina looked down, surprised. This was how things used to be between them, before he'd turned ten, before he'd joined the Young Pioneers, before he'd been taught to put Party over family.

She squeezed his hand back.

"Goodness," Mama said, pressing a hand to her

stomach. "That's quite a sensation, isn't it?" She was breathing fast. "Look at Moscow, children!"

They pressed their faces against the window, even Mama. As dawn rose, the city looked like a dollhouse village below, getting smaller by the minute. Nina rushed to try to identify places in the pink morning light, but everything looked different from above.

"There's Red Square!" Ivan said.

"And the Kremlin!" Mama added.

Nina's eyes were wide. They were really flying. Nothing beneath them except air and clouds. She touched the glass gently.

The airplane suddenly dipped, and Mama shrieked and Ivan pressed a hand to his mouth. Nina leaned back, closing her eyes. She tugged off her red kerchief, needing to breathe.

The airplane continued to bump, keeping them all on edge, but soon they were too high to see anything but clouds. The pilot explained that it would be a three-hour flight to the launch site in Kazakhstan.

Once the airplane coasted smoothly and silence filled the cabin, Nina rubbed the kerchief between her hands nervously.

Mama squeezed her hand as though reading her mind. "I am sure that your father and his colleagues are doing whatever they can to ensure Laika's safety."

"But the administrators told Papa to rush the design

of the rocket," Nina blurted out. "To take shortcuts if needed . . ."

Mama let out a deep breath. "When we arrive at the cosmodrome, you can speak with Papa about your worries."

Though Mama was acting brave, she looked troubled, too. Nina suspected that in her own way, Mama had also come to love the dog.

By the time they landed, the desire for the truth was burning a hole in Nina's throat. As soon as the airplane rolled to a stop and the pilots gave the all clear, she tumbled out of the small plane onto the runway, which was covered with a layer of sand. Everything was sand here: It coated her skin and found its way into her mouth and eyes. Despite the high midday sun, the wind was frigid without buildings to block it.

Reporters were waiting for them. Each wore an identification badge attached to his coat. Soldiers stood close by in case the reporters were tempted to wander somewhere they shouldn't.

Nina scanned the area for Papa, but all she could see were a few military trucks and the endless sand of the cold Kazakh desert.

"Have you come to cheer your hero dog to glory?" one of the reporters asked.

She gave him a hard glare. She knew the line the administrators wanted her to say: *Only the great Soviet Union, with its clever minds and brave hearts, could succeed at such a bold mission.* But she was tired of saying what they wanted her to say.

She announced, "I don't want a hero. I just want my dog." She whirled on the nearest soldier and demanded, "Where is the launch site?"

He pointed to the horizon, where she could make out a towering rocket through the blowing sand.

She started toward it, but the soldier rested a hand on her shoulder, holding her back. "Young lady, stop! It is three miles away!"

"I need to see my father. I need to ask him something right away."

The soldier pointed to a nearby truck. "We are to take you to the viewing platform. Come, he is waiting for you there."

23

LAIKA

THE PEOPLE IN WHITE COATS carried Laika and Albina into a facility that was all cold, hard surfaces, so different from the parlor's overstuffed armchairs. They clipped her fur short with a buzzing machine so powerful it even made her bones vibrate, then sponged a pungent yellow chemical over her skin. Her side ached from where they had bandaged it. As though he was aware of this, Tailor fitted the starflyer suit around her torso as gently as possible, though she still let out a whine of pain when he cinched the straps. He belted the leather harness around her shoulders and hips with equal care and attached the canvas bag she was meant to empty her bowels into.

Throughout it all, Albina remained in her crate, nose pressed against the air holes.

Wherever this cold room was, there were no Ink Men with flashing black boxes now. When Tailor picked her up to check her harness, she stole a glimpse out the window, where flat earth stretched as far as she could see.

Where was Good Girl? Wouldn't she say goodbye?

"Albina, I think it is time for me to go," Laika barked in a high voice toward the other dog's crate. "They've put me in the harness and attached the wires. All that's left is to go into the rocket. I don't think I can have a friend there." She hoped she sounded brave, though her words trembled.

"I'll see you again soon. I know it." Albina's voice echoed from her crate. Laika wished she could see her friend one more time, more than just a nose through an air hole.

"I'll be brave," Laika barked. "And you must be, too. Take care of Mushka until I get back."

"I will. I promise. Goodbye, my friend."

"Goodbye, Albina."

Tailor eased Laika into her travel crate, careful not to jostle any of the wires. She felt the crate swinging from side to side as he carried her . . . where? From the air holes, she glimpsed flashes of colors: the dusty brown earth, the white of Tailor's coat, and then a towering monolith of metal with stripes down the side. It was as tall as the tallest building in all of Moscow.

"*Rocket*," she breathed to herself.

She couldn't stop her limbs from shaking. She hadn't seen the Big Hats, but she picked up their scent everywhere: that oily, soapy smell. Regardless, she tilted her chin high like the dog in the poster, even if there was no one there to witness it but herself.

The crate jolted as the ground beneath them shifted. The hairs on the back of her neck rose. She and Tailor were moving *upward* somehow, like they had in the moving closet in Moscow. Machinery clanked and churned. Giant bars rose like the skeletal spine of a metal monster.

Then the upward movement stopped, and Tailor's boots clanked as he started walking again. He unlatched her crate, and sudden bright sunlight blinded her.

Her eyes soon adjusted, but she wasn't certain what she was looking at. She was high in the sky, in the realm of clouds. At the very top of the metal skeleton. There were no walls, only bars forming a sort of cage to hold them in. In front of her was a familiar sight: the capsule from the parlor.

"*Good girl,*" a familiar voice said.

Laika's tail perked up. Whiskers stroked her, careful of the bandage on her side. Soft Hands was behind him, holding two bowls. One contained water, which Laika gladly filled her dry throat with, and the other held the meat-smelling goo.

Soft Hands took her time emptying the bowl of goo into a special receptacle in the capsule for Laika to eat from later. When she turned around at last, there were tears in her eyes. Laika cocked her head. She leaned forward as far as her harness would allow her and pressed her nose into Soft Hands's palm. *What's wrong?* she wondered. Wasn't this a moment of celebration?

Careful of the sensors, Whiskers delicately placed Laika into the capsule. She immediately sat in the place and position that they had taught her. *See?* She wagged her tail at Whiskers. *I'm being a good girl. So that they don't lock you in a pound for people.* While Whiskers clipped a chain to Laika's harness to keep her in place, Laika studied the lines of his face, tried to find Good Girl in them. There was a particular heaviness to his features today. Even the prickly collection of hairs beneath his nose remained drooped.

He worked in silence, occasionally turning to Tailor or Soft Hands for a piece of equipment that he fitted into the walls of the capsule. The walls were covered with soft white cloth, like the blankets on Good Girl's bed. Laika closed her eyes, remembering that magical night. Once she was back, every night would be filled with magic.

But when she opened her eyes, she saw that Whiskers's face was even more grim. Tailor wouldn't look at Laika, even when she barked. The round space helmet was nowhere to be seen. Whiskers twisted a knob inside the capsule, and air began pouring in through a vent. She must not need the helmet in this particular capsule.

Tailor snugged up her harness. Soft Hands secured her food dish. Whiskers double-checked the hinges on the capsule door. Laika recognized that these were the same steps they had done before placing her in the Black Eternity.

This was it! The moment they'd all prepared for!

But why was Soft Hands crying? Why did Whiskers look sad? This was supposed to be the greatest trick any dog had ever done—to fly! This was supposed to win good things for Whiskers's family, wasn't it? Suddenly it wasn't so easy to be brave. It made her anxious that the people were acting strangely. *This mission isn't like the ones before*, Albina had explained, *where dogs return from the sky floating beneath cloths like clouds.* No dog had ever reached the stars before. It was the great Unknown.

Did the people know something she didn't?

"I'm not so sure about this anymore," Laika barked, though she knew the people in white coats didn't understand her. "Maybe we should go back to Star City. Maybe I should practice the tricks more." She knew she had to be strong for Good Girl—she had to do this—but sometimes a dog could only be so brave.

Whiskers looked stricken. He pinched the bridge of his nose. Then he took a deep breath and reached into his pocket. He slipped a small object into the capsule, where it was hidden from any of the other people in white coats.

Good Girl's blanket!

The smell of the blanket—of Good Girl—washed over Laika. Her muscles unclenched. Slowly, her breathing slowed to normal. This was the sign she had been waiting for. The sign that everything was okay.

Good Girl needs me to be strong, she reminded herself fiercely.

Whiskers leaned into the capsule and placed a soft kiss

on the end of Laika's nose. He murmured gentle words. His eyes seemed to carry the weight of every worry in the world.

He closed the capsule.

The clanking sound of massive latches being sealed echoed around her.

Laika's heart pounded fast again. The capsule's emptiness ate at her. *It's just like the Black Eternity*, she reminded herself. *I did it once and I can do it again.* A small round window allowed light in, but it was too high for her to see through. She pushed up to her hind legs, stretching as far as the chain would allow. On the other side of the window stretched the wide expanse of earth, the metal bones of the machine, and far below, a platform filled with Ink Men and Big Hats and soldiers who were so small they looked like ants.

She watched as Whiskers and Tailor disappeared into the metal bones of the tower, but Soft Hands remained behind. She set to work checking the pipes that supplied Laika's capsule with air. Laika scratched at the glass with her claws—*scratch scratch scratch*—but Soft Hands didn't look at her. Soft Hands closed her eyes and took a deep breath, then opened them and began working again.

Laika dropped her paws. She sat back down.

I'm supposed to be a good girl, she thought. *So that's what I'll be.*

She picked up her blanket and chewed.

The seconds stretched into minutes. The minutes stretched into hours.

Her haunches grew sore, but she was used to this—to waiting. Only this time they wouldn't take her out after a week and give her a sausage for mastering the trick. She was on her own now until the capsule landed back on Earth. It could be many days, for all she knew, or even longer. Maybe even until the snows ended, the flowers bloomed again.

As she waited, her vision filled with dreams, with the sounds of people cheering for her return amid a beautiful spring day.

Time to fly.

24

NINA

AS SOON AS THE MILITARY truck rolled to a stop, Nina threw open the door and raced out into the desert.

"Nina, wait!" Mama called, struggling with the suitcases.

The wind was frigid against Nina's cheeks. She hugged her blue coat tighter. Wooden planks formed a path from the parking area to the base of a giant viewing platform constructed out of metal scaffolding. Communist Party flags fluttered along the platform's railings. Administrators Bolshoi and Grom were already up there, shaking hands and pointing to the towering rocket. Even at three stories high, the viewing platform was dwarfed by the distant rocket. She had to shade her eyes to look up so high.

"Nina, come back!"

She ignored her mother's calls. Her new shoes pinched her feet, so she kicked them off and kept running over the planks. When she glanced back, Ivan had also climbed out of the truck and was running after her.

She reached the stairs. The metal was painfully cold on her socked feet, but she clenched her jaw and took the stairs as fast as her legs could carry her. Back and forth, up the flights until she was on top of the platform, where the wind whipped even more savagely.

She spotted him in the crowd. "Papa!"

Nina pushed her way through reporters who yelped in surprise, and a few who called after her for an interview. Papa was speaking with Director Sonin and the other scientists. His face looked like it had aged a year in the days that they'd been apart. He was dabbing at his neck like he was sweating, despite the cold. When he heard her, his face lit up.

"Nina!"

She crashed into him.

"You're here at last." His face broke into a smile. He looked over her shoulder. "Where are your mother and brother?"

"Papa, I need to speak with you right away."

His eyebrows rose.

"Ah, the children are here!" Comrade Bolshoi clapped his hands together. Comrades Bolshoi and Grom wore big smiles, but there was an impatience behind their eyes. "Excellent. We have time for a few photographs before the launch. Put on your red kerchief, Young Pioneer. Your face might be on the cover of *Pravda* tomorrow, and we want everyone to see the strength of your pride." He waved to the group of reporters. "Gentlemen, over here!"

Nina leaned close to Papa's ear and whispered urgently, "I need to ask you something. It's important."

Papa met her eyes, then nodded. "Comrades . . . if you'll excuse us for one moment."

The administrators' smiles faltered. Grom checked his watch. "The launch is scheduled to begin soon, comrade, and we need to record interviews . . ."

"This will only take a moment." Papa's voice was firm.

They frowned at his insistence but didn't object. Papa led Nina to the corner, near some empty seats, where they couldn't be overheard.

Nina stared at the rocket towering in the distance.

"It's so far away," she whispered. "I thought it would be closer."

Papa tilted her chin up so her eyes met his. "What's wrong, Nina?"

She took a deep breath. "There was a field trip at school to feed street dogs in honor of Laika. Papa, they were saying . . ." Her voice broke. "They said you can't bring Laika home."

The already heavy lines in Papa's face deepened. He rubbed the bridge of his nose, then took a breath that seemed to draw in every muscle in his body.

"Is it true?" she pressed.

His gaze shifted to his shoes.

She tugged on his arm. "Papa, tell me that you wouldn't send Laika to space without a way to bring her home!"

When Papa's eyes finally met hers, they were rimmed in red. "I pushed for more time. I told them the technology wasn't ready. But they insisted it happen now, before the New Year's celebration, to beat the Americans. I promise you, Nina, I tried to get more time."

She stared at him. Took a shaky step backward. "So it is true."

He tilted his head. "Lapochka, I told you before that difficult things are required of us. We are all called on to make great sacrifices for the Motherland."

"*We* aren't making any sacrifices," she insisted. "Laika is!"

Her heart pounded so hard she felt her temples throbbing. She watched the reporters snapping pictures of proud men and women in uniform with the rocket in the backdrop. She pressed a hand to her head. "Do they all know?"

Papa nodded reluctantly. "The administrators do. The reporters have not yet been told. We've been instructed to tell them that regardless of what happens, Laika is alive and well during the launch and for the following few days. The world will learn the truth eventually, but today is a day of triumph for the Soviet Union. A day when we warn our rivals not to trifle with us. A day when we make the impossible happen."

She shook her head, feeling bitter in the pit of her

stomach. What was triumphant about sending Laika up to die?

She felt tears pressing at her eyes, but then she brushed them away and gritted her teeth. "You have to stop the launch."

Papa's eyebrows shot up. "What did you say?"

She grabbed his arm. "You must, Papa. This isn't right."

He motioned to the distant rocket. "It's impossible. They've closed off the support structure except for essential personnel. The controls are in the hands of the Chief Designer now. There is no stopping the launch."

She gripped his arm harder. "If we can't stop the rocket, maybe we can get Laika out. We can't let her go on a mission with no chance of return. She isn't like the rest of the equipment you have in that capsule. She's a living creature."

He pressed a hand to his chest as though he, too, felt a stab deep in his chest.

"Papa!"

They turned to find Ivan breathing heavily from the run up the stairs. He hurried over to them, his face red and blotchy. "Is it true, Papa? I don't want Laika to die."

Papa rubbed his temples, looking devastated. "This mission is orchestrated to prove our superiority in the eyes of the world. Isn't that what you told the Chief Designer you wanted, Ivan? Victory for the Motherland?"

Ivan wiped a hand over his face. He looked younger than ten, just a schoolboy in a uniform half a size too big.

"I don't care about that anymore, Papa. I'm sorry I ever did."

Mama reached the top of the stairs, breathing hard. Her hair was disheveled. She'd kicked off her high heels, too, and was in stocking feet. She rushed over.

"Lidia, they want to save the dog," Papa said.

Mama's face was also splotched with red. She bit her lip. "Children, there is nothing we can do. They will label us traitors. Accuse us of sabotaging the launch to help the Americans. Your father and I could be sent to the labor camps."

Papa drew in a long breath, his face conflicted, as he turned to Mama. "Lidia, if they want to send us to the labor camps, they will. They do not need a reason when a lie will do just as well."

Nina raked her fingers through her hair. She didn't want her parents to be arrested, didn't want Ivan and herself shipped to a state orphanage. Maybe Ludmilla's family had been right to run when they had the chance.

But Nina didn't *want* to run.

"This is our home," she stated. "This is the land of the firebird, of the Bukavac. Aren't we always saying how brave Russians are? How can we call ourselves brave if we don't voice the truth? If we can send a dog to die and call it victory?"

Mama pressed a hand to her mouth, letting out a silent sob. Ivan was sniffling, too. Papa reached out and took Ivan's and Nina's hands. "The children are right. What

kind of prison will we live in, in our hearts, if we do this
to the dog?"

They all looked to Mama.

Mama let out another quiet sob, then ran a hand-
kerchief over her face. Resolutely, she took Nina's and
Ivan's free hands so that the four of them stood in a circle,
holding one another tightly for the first time in a long
time.

Papa squeezed their hands. "Let's try to save her."

25

LAIKA

THOUGH IT HAD BEEN FREEZING outside, the air inside the capsule was hot and stuffy. Laika leaned toward the pipe that pumped in oxygen, lapping up air greedily. Heat radiated off the churning machinery. Small fans blew down on her, but they weren't strong enough to do more than stir the stagnant air. The equipment fastened to the walls blinked with bright lights. She had her blanket, but not even chewing the soft fabric gave much relief now. Her attention went from the receptacle of gelatinous food, to the clanking machines, to the small round window.

Waiting, waiting, waiting.

She broke into a pant. Her breath felt heavy. The reflection on the mirrored machines showed a distorted dog with too-big eyes, the whites flashing like the startled Warm Dogs in Moscow who weren't used to noise and cars and cold. Her stomach was churning as fast as the fans. It was still daylight outside, not a star in the sky. If it were night, what would the Dog Star tell her to do? *Be brave, be brave, little one.* But Laika's limbs were shaking and she couldn't make them stop. A big light bulb suddenly lit up and she whined, frightened. The inside of the capsule was coated in flickering light like the world was burning. It was getting harder to picture the waiting crowds cheering her return. What if something went wrong?

The light bulb shut off without warning.

Laika stood on her hind legs once more to look out the round window. The view hadn't changed. Metal bones and the flat, bare earth beyond. She wondered how her life would be different if she'd had a pack leader as a pup, like Good Girl had with Whiskers. She'd lost her mother and siblings to the dogcatcher when she could barely bark. She had spent her whole life alone, believing that was the only way to survive.

How wrong she had been. The world could be bleak, but it could also be beautiful.

But wait! What was that?

On the platform far below the rocket, Laika saw a flash of blue, blue like the sky. A coat. A girl.

Laika's breath caught.

Good Girl.

She pressed her paw to the window, her nails curved against the glass that kept them apart.

26

NINA

NINA'S HEART RACED AS PAPA led the family toward the stairs. His eyes were still rimmed in red, but the heavy lines in his face had eased.

"We mustn't raise any suspicion," he said in a low voice, careful not to be overheard. "At the same time, we must hurry. The launch sequence is scheduled to begin in twenty-two minutes. That's when all the technicians remaining on the support scaffolding will have to evacuate to a safe distance. Since there is no way to stop the launch, our only option is to sneak Laika out of the capsule. I will need you three to cause a distraction down here so I can go up in the elevator." He looked at his family. "Any ideas?"

Nina thought of what could possibly distract well-trained soldiers. Her eyes lit up. "Ivan, do you remember the game of War in the park? Dima had a maneuver to get himself chased so that I could slip by. At least that's how it was supposed to work."

Ivan nodded eagerly. "I remember."

Mama pressed her hands against the back of Nina's and Ivan's coats. "Be careful, you two! Make it look like a disagreement between siblings, nothing more. Nina, say that Ivan stole your kerchief and you are chasing him to get it back. We want them to think you are only foolish children and take you back to the viewing platform. I'll be there waiting for you."

Nina nodded. She clutched the railing and followed her mother and father. Her heart ticked as fast as a clock, counting down the time.

"Stop." A soldier at the bottom of the stairs raised a stiff hand. He frowned at the family, his eyes dropping to Nina's and Mama's dirty stocked feet. "Safety protocol. All personnel and authorized guests must remain on the viewing platform. The launch sequence will soon begin."

Papa's mouth opened, but nothing came out. He'd always been bad at lying, which was one of the things Nina loved best about him. Now, though, she wished he had learned more from his Party comrades.

At his silence, Mama grabbed Nina's and Ivan's hands. "The children need to use the toilet!" *Mama* understood how lies worked.

The soldier gave a hard shake of his head. "They will have to wait."

Mama snorted. "You must not have children, comrade. When they say they need to go, they need to *go*. I don't believe it would look good for the Motherland if all the photographs show Young Pioneers who have wet their pants during Russia's finest hour."

The soldier turned a shade paler. "The restroom is on the way to the hangar by the runway. Hurry back."

Mama dragged the children in the direction of the airplane runway. As soon as they were safely around the corner, hidden from view, Papa clapped his hands. "Bravo, Lidia! Now follow me, all of you. We'll have to go under the platform scaffolding to reach the rocket. They will be too suspicious if they see children near the launch structure."

They kept hidden in the dark belly of the scaffolding as they ducked their way under the beams. When they reached the end, Papa held out a hand, motioning for them to wait. The base of the rocket service structure was about a hundred feet away, over open desert, where anyone looking down would see them. Papa pointed to a military truck parked between them and the rocket.

"On the count of three, we run to the truck, yes?"

They nodded.

He held up his fingers. One. Two. Three.

One after another, they darted across the rocky sand to the far side of the truck. The wind was bitter and unforgiving. Nina was breathing fast. She pitched her head up to look at the rocket towering overhead.

Hold on, Laika, she thought. *We're coming.*

"There's the base of the service structure," Papa said. "See there, the elevator? I need you to distract those two soldiers so I can start riding it up before they can stop me."

"But what about the stairs, Papa?" Nina asked. "They will follow you."

"By the time they climb them, I will have already gotten Laika. I'll hide her in my coat."

"Konstantin," Mama said. "Wait. You'll get in trouble when they realize you've entered the tower without permission." She pinched the skin at her throat, thinking. "We can tell them you realized there was a problem with the capsule . . ." Her eyes lit up. "You needed to address it and there was no time to ask permission!"

"Yes, that's perfect, Lidia," Papa said.

Nina glanced at her brother. What if the plan didn't work? Would they be expelled from school for trespassing in a restricted area? Or worse?

Ivan grabbed her hand. At only ten, he was braver than most of the administrators with medals on their uniforms. "I'm ready."

She squeezed his hand. "Let's play War."

Ivan took a deep breath and ran toward the launch structure base. Nina charged after him, yelling loudly about him stealing her kerchief. She tried not to think about the dizzying height and the thin red bars of the rocket structure above them. Ahead, the two young soldiers flanking the elevator entrance straightened with surprise to see the children.

"Stop!" one yelled.

Ivan ignored them and kept running away from Nina.

"Stop! You children, this is no time for play!" One of the soldiers lunged for Ivan, and he let himself be caught just like Dima had during the game of War. Ivan glanced back at her.

Her turn.

She darted to the left, then pivoted, leading the other soldier away so that Papa could reach the elevator. "You— stop!" the soldier yelled, but she kept running as fast as she could. She heard his footsteps crunch in the sand. She circled back toward the platform, her lungs burning. After a moment she realized she didn't hear footsteps behind her anymore. She skidded to a stop and dared a look over her shoulder.

The second soldier had returned to the elevator and was speaking sharply to Papa, one hand on his intercom. Nina gasped. The soldier must have spied Papa and doubled back! Maybe the second soldier had played War as a Young Pioneer and recognized the trick.

Papa met her eyes with regret and shook his head. The soldier was already speaking into his intercom, probably requesting help. There was no way Papa could make it to the capsule.

She tipped her head up at the dizzyingly tall metal structure. The elevator shaft ran up ten stories, the elevator already rising to the top—Papa must have pressed the button but not been able to get inside before it started moving. Next to the elevator shaft, a steep set of utility stairs led to the top.

Before fear could get in her way, she ran for the stairs.

"Stop!" the guards called out sharply.

But one was holding Ivan and the other was with Papa. The one with the intercom seemed to consider running after her, but then he glanced at Papa and must have assumed he was more of a concern than a girl. He said into the intercom, "I need help at the tower base, now!"

Nina didn't let herself stop to think. She grabbed the handrail and started running up the stairs.

"Nina, don't!" Papa yelled. "It isn't safe!"

Nina ignored him. They couldn't throw a twelve-year-old girl into a labor camp, could they? Mama would come up with a story to save her, claim she was trying to be brave somehow. She climbed the stairs as fast as she could. Three flights. Four. Soon soldiers would be after her, but she had a head start on the stairs, and the slow-moving elevator would have to finish making it to the top of the tower, then descend again. She raced up the stairs, huffing, until her legs burned.

Seven flights.

Eight!

At last she reached the top. She leaned over to catch her breath. The staircase and elevator opened onto the tower's roof, which was connected to the rocket by a narrow bridge.

At the end of the bridge, Svetlana was crouching by

the capsule door, packing away her toolbox, preparing to evacuate. The round window of Laika's capsule winked in the sun.

Nina sucked in a breath. She was so close!

When Svetlana heard the noise, she looked up in surprise and her mouth fell open. "Nina? You can't be here!"

A red alarm started blaring. Nina leaned over the railing and looked back down at the tower below. The elevator had reached the bottom and soldiers were climbing on. She could hear another soldier clanking up the stairs, fast.

Nina grabbed the handrails and shakily made her way across the bridge towering ten stories above the desert. Svetlana stood up, shaking her head. "Nina—"

Nina reached the end of the bridge, which was latched to Laika's capsule with giant metal pins. She grabbed the heavy handle of the capsule and tugged on it, but it didn't open.

"Nina, stop!" Svetlana grabbed her wrist away from the capsule. "What has happened? Where is Konstantin?"

"I have to open the hatch!"

"I already bolted it shut." Svetlana pointed to the big round bolts surrounding the hatch door.

Nina shook her head anxiously. "Open it again! We have to get Laika out. She'll die if they send her up there."

Svetlana blinked, searching for words. "Yes. I know. But *we* will be sent to the labor camps if we free her!"

Nina grabbed Svetlana's hand, looking into her eyes. "Papa says no one has to know. He can alter the data to make it seem like Laika is still inside. He was going to smuggle her out in his coat, but he was caught by the guards, so I came . . ."

Svetlana's eyebrows shot up. "Oh. Oh."

They both looked at Laika through the glass, her mouth open and panting happily to see Nina. Then Svetlana's face shifted to one of determination.

"No. Impossible. That plan will never work."

Nina started to protest, but Svetlana quickly added, "Even if Konstantin altered the reports to imply that the dog was still there, the rocket is carefully calibrated to her weight. If the capsule is suddenly twelve pounds lighter, it could veer off course and the administrators will know we interfered." For a moment, they stood on top of the tower in tense silence. Svetlana could be arrested if she helped, could lose her job and her standing with the Party. But then the look on Svetlana's face changed to one of determination. She turned back to her toolbox. She hefted it a few times and then took out a few tools and a hand scale. She hooked up the toolbox to the scale and weighed it. "Laika weighs 12.1 pounds, and this is 12.2 pounds. Close enough that it won't throw off the equipment. We'll swap out my toolbox for the dog."

Nina felt tears of relief in the corners of her eyes.

Svetlana turned to the hatch and began twisting open the bolts with a wrench.

Laika, inside the capsule, strained against the chain holding her in place, her tail wagging wildly.

Nina pressed her hands against the glass and breathed, "Hold on, Laika."

Laika's tongue hung out as she scratched a paw against the glass. Nina wanted so badly to hold the dog. There was little chance of smuggling her out in a coat with the soldiers after them, but Laika could still escape. She'd seen Laika run around Star City's courtyard—she was fast. And years on the streets had taught her how to evade attackers. She'd have no trouble dodging the hands of the soldiers and darting down the long staircase to the bottom, where she'd have the freedom of the desert. She'd find her way to civilization, she'd find water and food somehow, and she'd *survive*.

A deep rumble came from behind them, and Nina turned in time to see the elevator doors opening. A soldier stepped out, intercom in hand. When his eyes settled on Nina, he pressed the button. "I see the girl. I'm bringing her down now."

He started across the bridge.

27

LAIKA

GOOD GIRL WAS SO CLOSE—just on the other side of the window!

Laika had never wagged her tail so furiously before. Suddenly the stuffy air inside the capsule felt lighter, the pain in her side disappeared. When Good Girl was close, everything was better.

Laika gave another happy bark. She knew Good Girl wouldn't forget to say goodbye. She had climbed that enormous tower just to wish Laika well on her journey. Panting from the heat, Laika scratched a paw against the glass. What she would give for a final back scratch from the girl, but she supposed that would have to wait until her return.

So much had changed since her days huddled in a broken shoe crate, eating skin-and-bone mice. Back then, she hadn't known the joy of a full stomach. Of friends like

Albina and Mushka. Of warm sausage given by a woman with the softest hands she'd ever felt. Of belly rubs. And most of all, of Good Girl. Good Girl had shown her the magic of picture books. Of games of fetch. Of warm fires. Of solyanka soup! Of spending an entire night in the arms of a girl who held her with a love she'd never experienced, a love rivaled only by the Dog Star's bountiful light.

Through the window, Laika saw a man step out of the giant metal box and say something sharp. Good Girl's face suddenly turned frightened. She yelled like she was hurt, even though the man hadn't touched her. Tears began to spill down Good Girl's face.

Laika's ears rose, on alert. She cocked her head.

Was Good Girl sad to say goodbye? Had the soldiers been cruel to her? Threatened to put Whiskers in the people pound?

I'll come back, she thought. *I won't leave you.* She took her paw away from the window, then sat down in the capsule as she had been trained to.

I'm a good girl, she told herself.

Soft Hands, standing by the hatch, pressed a hand against her chest. Tears were rolling down her cheeks, too.

I'll be back, Laika barked to reassure her. *I'll see you soon.*

Outside the capsule, an alarm was blaring. The soldier strode across the bridge and grabbed the tool out of Soft Hands's grasp, and then grabbed Good Girl's wrist. But she broke free and ran to the capsule. She pressed her face against the glass, smearing it with her tears.

Laika saw herself reflected in Good Girl's eyes, saw the same love there that she felt for Good Girl.

Don't be afraid, she barked. *I'll be brave. And you be brave, too.*

And then, all too soon, the soldier hauled Good Girl away.

28

NINA

ON THE EMPTY STEPPES OF Kazakhstan, the air still burned with smoke.

Cheers erupted from the administrators, who slapped one another on the back, and the military officials, who smoothed their hair that had been blown out of place by the launch, and the band, which pumped away vigorously at the Soviet anthem.

No one noticed the twelve-year-old girl with tearstained cheeks standing to the side of the viewing platform a safe distance from the cosmodrome. She wore her papa's thick brown coat, with its Institute of Space Medicine embroidery on the pocket, over her own blue one. In her arms hung a limp flag that someone had thrust into her hand for a photograph, but she wasn't concerned with the flag.

Her crying face was turned toward the sky.

"Laika," she said. "Fly true."

29

LAIKA

DURING HER TIME IN THE Black Eternity, Laika had learned that hours could pass as swiftly as minutes, or else drag on for what felt like days. Now the seconds ticked by on a machine strapped to the wall, matching the beating of her heart. She wouldn't curl up and go to sleep this time. Not that she *could* sleep—she was too alert, her panting heavy, her paws scratching the floor. The harness kept her from getting to an itch on her belly. She whined quietly. At one point, her rear end had felt a familiar need and she'd had no choice but to move to a corner of the capsule and empty her bowels into the canvas bag.

Through the window, she could no longer see any people.

The light bulb began to flash again.

The capsule was bathed in light that flickered on and off with the ticking of the machine. She pawed at her eyes, trying to shield them from the light. A sudden roar burst from another one of the machines and she jumped. The fur on her back rose.

The capsule began to rumble.

She felt the vibrations in the pads of her feet first. They trembled up through the metal floor, coming from somewhere deep below in the rocket. This, too, was familiar from the Shake-Shake Box. She lifted one paw, then another. But the vibrations spread from the floor to the walls, rattling the machinery. The ticking box began clanking in a way that didn't seem right. The vibrations turned to tremors that unsteadied her feet and made her stomach flop. She crouched low to the ground as she'd learned to do in the Shake-Shake Box. The ticking machine on the wall suddenly fell off its hook, smashing to the floor. Laika jumped. Her heart seemed to have a life of its own, sprinting faster and faster. She sniffed the fallen machine—a hint of smoke but no flame. The rest of the machinery rattled harder. The goo in her food receptacle was jiggling wildly.

She panted hard—the capsule was getting warmer, fast.

She moved toward the air vent. Drool dotted the floor beneath her lolling tongue. One of the rattling machines had a metal arm that was moving quickly toward the far end of a scale. The intense heat seemed to come from somewhere below. She shifted from side to side anxiously. The light bulb stopped its flashing and burned constantly now.

A sudden earsplitting burst of sound exploded from somewhere below. Laika started barking out of instinct, snapping at the scary noise. *Bark! Bark! Bark!* The capsule was thrashing. Laika's vision went blurry. The sound roared.

Be brave! she told herself.

She hunkered low as she had been trained to do in the Spinning Storm. *Focus. Adjust.* The chains and harness rubbed at her neck. The wires attached to her skin tangled around her limbs. The light burned brighter. The heat was stifling. Hotter even than steam grates during a muggy Moscow summer. So warm the air clogged her throat like chunks of mouse fur.

The vibrations made her stomach turn as drool pooled in her mouth. Through her blurry vision, she tried to focus on the black bolts circling the window.

She felt the capsule rise.

There was a feeling of separation, of leaving Earth. Her stomach churned at the unfamiliar sensation. The roar died down, though the walls still shook. She felt herself swaying and dug her claws in deeper, determined to remain steady.

The light clicked off.

She was plunged into darkness except for a few blinking buttons and the light from the window. Her haunches were twitching, but she forced them to move toward the window. Using all her strength, she lifted herself to look outside.

The view beyond was a blur. Flashes of blue sky and blinding lights. There—the ground! It was rapidly disappearing below her in a smear of brown. Her little heart started thumping faster. The sensor beeped in time with it.

She was doing it! She was flying!

Her rocket soared away from Earth like a bird taking off from the top of a building. The vibrations rattled her to the bone, but *she was flying*. She let out quick breaths that fogged the glass. Now it had all been worth it—the cages, the tricks. She remembered the dog on the poster and tipped up her chin. Good Girl would be proud of her. Good Girl would run up to the rocket when she returned to Earth and hold her and hold her and hold her and never let her go.

Outside the window, blue sky faded into black.

It was as though she was flying directly into the Nighttime. It had to be some kind of magic. How could night fall so quickly? Soon stars winked in the distant black. She forgot about the awful vibrations rumbling up her paws.

Suddenly, magically, her ears rose. They rose on their own toward the ceiling as though invisible hands held them up. Her body felt lighter, and she was pulled upward as surely as if Good Girl had lifted her into her arms. Laika's fur ruffled upward. The tubes attached to her heart floated into the air, dancing like butterflies in the grass. She tried to scratch the floor but her nails, somehow, no longer touched the ground. Her paws pushed against the glass and she found herself floating backward into the center of the capsule, as far as her harness chain would allow.

Not only was the rocket flying—so was she!

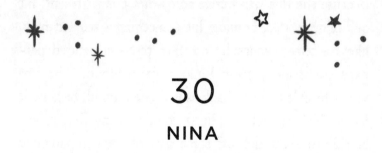

30

NINA

The Australian Women's Weekly
Wed 20 Nov 1957

LAIKA "PUPNIK" IN THE SKY
By RONALD McKIE

THE experiences of Laika ("Little Barker") are the strangest ever to happen to a dog. If she puts out her tongue, it won't loll wet and happy like the tongue of any well-adjusted dog on Earth. Oh, no. It will stick out straight and will loll only if she bends it down herself and keeps it there. And worse—it won't drip. If she picks up a bone and then drops it, as even the best-behaved dog will do, the bone won't drop. Not a bit of it. The bone will stay in front of her suspended right in front of her nose. And if she scratches, an act all normal dogs and humans enjoy, and kicks out a flea, that flea will be much more bewildered than Laika. Why? Because the flea will hurtle across her compartment, hit one of the sides, bounce, hit something else, and may, like the bone, eventually come to rest—suspended perhaps yards away from Laika's warm blood. The flea won't be able to walk back as it floats around, because it has nothing to walk on, but if it's a cunning flea, it may be able to get a kick off some part of the compartment and perhaps propel itself back toward the dog, though there is no certainty that it would ever reach her.

This description of what could be happening to Laika comes from Dr. John Piddington, the C.S.I.R.O. Radio physicist and authority on the upper atmosphere, who some weeks ago helped explain Sputnik II to our readers. "On Monday, November 4," he told me, "when my wife read that Sputnik II was circling the world every 102 minutes, she didn't give a thought to the fantastic scientific and technological achievement of the Russians. All she could say was, 'But what's happening to the little dog?'"

31

LAIKA

LAIKA'S MOUTH HUNG OPEN, HER tongue lolling. The strange magic made her feel weightless, like the sleek silver fish that floated in the river that ran through the city. Her ears hung suspended in air as she drifted toward the padded wall, tethered only by the harness chain. She reached out a paw to touch the air vent. Her nails grazed it as she continued to float by. She bumped up against a blinking machine and managed to push off with her snout, sending her drifting toward the floor upside down. Her heart flip-flopped and her feet scrambled, catching nothing but air. The chain tugged. Then she bumped headfirst into the window. How did birds control the wind as they did? She floated near the receptacle of goo and strained her chin and stuck out her tongue and managed to get a small lick.

Then her eyes caught on something familiar. Something sky blue. Her blanket!

The blanket was floating, too! Its tattered strings fanned out in all directions as it spun in lazy circles toward the window. Laika's heart soared. Her rear foot managed to push off from the window and she angled herself toward the knotted blanket with her jaws open.

Yes!

Her teeth closed around the edge of the fabric triumphantly. She pawed the air again, this time out of pleasure. She clenched her jaws tightly around this small piece of Good Girl. Was Good Girl still standing on the platform in the desert? Had she cheered when Laika's rocket rose to the sky? She wished Good Girl could be here, too, floating through the air like the river fish, while outside the window the world had become night.

She felt a sudden tug in her heart.

She hoped the rocket would return soon. She already missed Good Girl. She kept remembering the girl's tears, the girl's fears.

One of the machines started beeping loudly on the wall. Laika churned her feet in the air to see it. A white light flashed beneath a dial whose arm was rapidly sweeping from one end to the other. A hiss started from the floor, followed by a burst of hot steam. Alarmed, Laika twisted toward the air vent, but it was out of reach on the other side of the capsule. The white light burned brighter, followed by a shrill alarm like the trucks that raced through the streets of Moscow when the building across the street had caught fire.

What was happening?

The light blazed with even more intensity. Laika panted. Everything was white. Everything was blinding.

Too hot! Too bright!

Her vision blurred. The heat made her dizzy. Her heart was beating fast, faster than it ever had, and a little voice inside her head told her that it was as fast as a heart could possibly beat.

A sudden fear sank its teeth into her.

Is this the White Sleep?

No dog ever woke from the White Sleep. It was the sleep that came after too much hunger, after too cold a night. If this *was* the White Sleep, when the rocket returned to Earth, she wouldn't be there to greet Good Girl with a bark and a jump. It was just like Albina had said: This mission wasn't like the others. The people in white coats had never done this before. Something might go wrong.

Steam shot out in bursts from the floor. Now all the alarms in the capsule were blaring, every light blinking a warning. The white light drowned them all out. Laika pawed her way through the air toward the window, Good Girl's blanket safely clenched in her mouth.

I can't sleep the White Sleep, she thought. *I promised Good Girl I'd come back!*

Good Girl was waiting for her somewhere far below. So were Whiskers and Soft Hands and Tailor, whose lives depended on Laika's mission succeeding. So were Albina and Mushka. They were her pack now, and she'd fight tooth and claw to return to them.

She pressed her nose against the window. The stars dazzled in her blurry vision.

"I tried to be good," she whispered. "I tried to be brave."

Her bark came out as a weak, thin sound. When she tried to bark again, she couldn't.

As the blanket floated gently away, Laika focused on the stars outside. How many nights had she huddled in her cold alley in Moscow, gazing up at these very stars?

Then a shift occurred in the world.

Laika felt a strange tingle throughout her limbs. It was like the sensation of floating but a hundred times more magical. Beyond the round capsule window, Laika saw that the white light that had been so scary at first now transformed into small dots of light. *It's only the stars!* she realized. Her fear began to melt away. How had she mistaken the beautiful stars for blaring lights and alarms?

One star burned brighter than the rest. It filled the capsule with a light that drowned out the taste of goo in her mouth, the smell of chemicals, the rumbling of machines. She felt the light seep through her skin all the way to her marrow, deeper than it ever had before.

Welcome home, little one, the Dog Star said.

"This is home?"

All dogs have a home amid the stars, here with me in the light, if they want one.

"Am I a Warm Dog now?"

Now and forever.

Laika felt the white light overtake her. Through the magic of the Nighttime, the entire capsule faded away, and she was floating outside the hatch, outside everything, floating in the beautiful black sky toward the light of the Dog Star, who was waiting to embrace her. She was somehow *in* the Nighttime now, part of it, and the Nighttime was where magic happened. Not even birds reached such heights. Not the people's flying machines. Nothing did— only a dog brave enough to chase the stars.

A soft object bobbed against her side, smelling of soup.

My blanket!

Memories rushed back to her. Lapping up solyanka soup. Playing fetch in the back alley. Sleeping a whole night pressed against Good Girl's steadily beating heart. Laika suddenly scrambled away from the white light, pawing at the dark.

"Wait—I can't stay. I have to go back. I have a mission!"

You've gone farther than any dog ever has. You've accomplished more than a dog from the streets ever dreamed of. Be proud, little one. The world will benefit from the sacrifices you've made. Without you, humanity might never have left the Earth.

"But Albina came back . . . so many of the starflyers came back."

A deep whine of loss rumbled within her chest. She'd known this mission was dangerous, but she'd always kept alive the belief that at the end of it she'd be in Good Girl's arms.

She let out a deep, anguished howl toward the blackness.

The Dog Star radiated out light in return.

And perhaps you will. Here in the stars, time is not the same as it was for you before. Dogs' lives have a way of circling back. If a dog is strongly pulled to Earth, to a girl or a boy or mission, then sometimes that dog finds a way back. A new body, but the same soul. You will remember her. You will see her again, if you truly believe.

Laika blinked into the light. She thought of the pictures in Good Girl's book of the man who had ridden on a wolf's back. The world was filled with wondrous and strange things. "I do," she whispered. "I believe."

She continued to float through the endless night toward the Dog Star's light.

But first, little one, it is time for you to rest, and be warm, and be loved, and to shine your light on others.

Something glowed from within Laika's body. The warmth in her bones spread to every part of her body, her tail and her paws and the tip of her ears, and as she stretched out her paws toward the heavens, she burst with the light of her own inner star.

EPILOGUE

NINA

ALONE IN MOSCOW, NINA CURLED up in her bed. Tears dampened her pillow and the dark tangles of her hair. She'd cried until she couldn't cry any more. It was a cold, clear night, the kind of night that called to something deep inside her to throw open the window and stare at the moon, but she didn't have the heart to get out of bed.

Their family hadn't spoken much on the journey home from Baikonur Cosmodrome. After the launch, the administrators had dragged Papa to an interrogation chamber, where they'd questioned him for hours. Nina and Ivan and their mother had sat outside on a bench, guarded by soldiers with rifles, as all kinds of horrors filled Nina's mind. But then the door had opened. Papa looked rumpled and pale, but they had let him and Svetlana go.

"Congratulations again, Comrade Azarov," Comrade

Bolshoi said gruffly, slapping him a little too hard on the back.

On the flight home, Papa explained that Director Sonin had told the administrators that Papa had been acting on mistaken information and that he'd been trying to *save* the mission from a faulty door lock. The administrators hadn't believed it, of course. But Papa guessed they couldn't risk the truth coming out: that another one of their scientists had gone against orders. Sergei Sokolov's betrayal was still too much of a black mark on the space administration. So they'd swallowed the lie, and instead of sending Papa to a labor camp, they'd pretended everything had been a complete success. Papa had been showered with praise. Pats on the back. And then back in Moscow, cigars and champagne were sent to their house for reporters to see. Radio broadcasts from around the world told of the hero of Moscow, Laika the cosmonaut dog, the starflyer, who had opened the door for humanity's exploration of space.

Whenever those broadcasts had come on, Mama had gently switched the radio off.

Now, Nina heard the sound of crying from the next bedroom over.

She climbed out of bed and knocked softly on her brother's door. "Ivan?"

"Nina?"

She opened the door. He was sitting up in bed, looking out the window at the night sky. He brushed some tears away. "I couldn't sleep."

She felt an urge to start crying again herself, but she needed to be brave for her brother. She sat on the corner of his bed. "I miss her, too."

Downstairs, they could hear Mama and Papa speaking in quiet voices, finishing off the zharkoye stew Mama had made and discussing a trip to visit relatives the following month. Papa must have found a bone in his stew—a sign of luck—because Mama laughed.

Ivan shook his head. "Before the night Laika came home, I can't remember the last time I heard Mama laughing."

Nina nodded. "I know."

She only remembered her mother being nervous, careful. And Papa spending such long nights at work. Something changed the night Laika came home. In a way, the little dog had been magic. But not magic like the circus fortune-teller's act. Real magic. When Nina had listened to the radio that afternoon, it was like the whole world had stopped their disagreements to celebrate Laika. The radio host spoke of how the dog's journey was the crucial first step toward sending a human into space, then to the moon, then into a universe full of possibility, leading to technology that would change the world—things like satellites that could connect people from all different countries and all different languages. Because of Laika, they said, a daring, bold, beautiful future might be within reach.

Nina whispered, "I'll never forget her as long as I live."

Ivan started crying again, and Nina wrapped her arms

around him. After a few minutes, he rubbed his nose and laid his head on his pillow, and soon he was breathing heavily, asleep.

Nina looked out the bedroom window at the night sky. The lights of Moscow sometimes made it hard to see the stars, but tonight they were out in full force. One shone most brightly of all, twinkling so strongly that Nina felt the light of it even in the little bedroom. Another, smaller star shone beside it. She'd never noticed this star before. Its light was different, warmer, and she watched the star until her eyelids began to close, too.

She dreamed of a dog who played fetch with the stars, who howled in the light of the moon, who had shown the world what love and bravery truly meant. A dog who, she believed in her heart, she would hold again.

That night and many after, in cities and apartments and houses around the world, millions of people woke up in the middle of the night to step outside and look overhead to see the light of the famous starflyer dog's satellite as it traveled through the sky. A satellite so bright that the only brighter light in the heavens was Sirius, the Dog Star. A beacon for anyone who had ever marveled up at the night sky in wonder, dreaming of the possibilities amid the stars.

AUTHOR'S NOTE

I first heard about Laika ten years ago when I stumbled upon
her photograph in a book. Instantly, I (like so many others) was
captivated by the brave spirit in her eyes. When I found out the
tragic end to her story, I felt heartbroken and angry, while at
the same time unable to let go of the wonder of what this small
dog from the streets of Moscow accomplished—being the first
living being to orbit the Earth. When I read more about her
story and learned that her trainers had sincere respect for her
and the other dogs, I felt overcome with questions of morality. I
spent five years trying to write Laika's story, afraid I was either
presenting the story too judgmentally about the scientists, or
not judgmentally enough. Ultimately, I decided to simply tell
the true story, which had so moved me, and let my readers feel
the wide range of emotions that might come. Hers is a sad story,
but also a triumphant one.

TRUTH VS. FICTION: LAIKA'S REAL STORY

Dog Star is a work of fiction, but the story of Laika is true. I
changed the human character names and some details of the
space program, including the timeline and the description of
her capsule, but the essence of Laika's story is here on the page.

She was real. She was sent into space. The whole world was fascinated by her journey and mourned her when she didn't return home.

Laika was one of many dogs found on the streets of Moscow by scientists working for the Institute of Space Medicine. As in the story, Soviet scientists decided to use dogs instead of monkeys after visiting a circus, though in reality the Soviet Union, also called the USSR, had used dogs for space research since the 1940s. Oleg Gazenko, one of the dog trainers, said, "The Americans are welcome to their flying monkeys; we're more partial to dogs." For the starflyer program, they chose dogs that weighed around eleven pounds (so they would fit in the small rockets), that were white or light colored (so they would show up well on video recordings used to transmit their conditions during launch), and female (because male dogs lift their leg to urinate, which wouldn't work with their space suits). They also specifically wanted dogs that were used to harsh conditions.

The depictions of Laika's training—and that of Albina and Mushka, who were also real dogs—are very close to the actual training the Soviet space dogs underwent, including being fitted for space suits and space helmets; taught to withstand confined spaces, vibrations, and centrifugal force; and trained to eat a gelatinous form of food. They were even given press training to teach them how to interact with radio interviewers and photographers.

Many of Russia's historic churches and palaces, such as Petroff Palace, were commandeered by the Communist Party and used by the Soviet Air Force for training, so it would have been quite possible for space dogs to have trained there, too; however, by the late 1950s, the space dog program had moved to Star City, a large military compound outside Moscow. It is unlikely that a girl like Nina would have been allowed to work at the top secret facility or visit the cosmodrome to watch a launch, but there were occasions when Young Pioneers were invited to tour the Star City grounds. Though I depicted the scenes of *Dog Star* to take place in the winter, in reality, Laika's launch happened November 3, 1957.

From their journals and reports, it is clear that the Institute of Space Medicine scientists had great respect for their canine subjects and called them "colleagues," never "test subjects" or "experimental animals." While the space program was highly dangerous, most of the dogs sent into suborbital and orbital flight survived their missions and returned safely to Earth. Many of the dog cosmonauts were later adopted by their handlers and went on to live long, happy lives.

Unfortunately, Laika was not one of the dog survivors. The initial official Soviet report claimed that Laika survived for four days orbiting the Earth before she was painlessly euthanized with poisoned food. However, it's unclear whether scientists had the technology to do so from the ground at that time, and historians now believe it is more likely that Laika died from overheating just a few hours after launch.

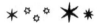

I still don't understand who I am: the first human
or the last dog in space.
—Yuri Gagarin, 1961

THE "SPACE RACE" BETWEEN THE SOVIET UNION AND THE UNITED STATES

The Soviet Union was a group of eastern European nations controlled by a single socialist government from 1922 to 1991. In the 1950s, the Soviet Union went through a period of rapid economic and industrial development, which placed it as a "superpower" rival to the United States, particularly when it came to the two countries' different political philosophies.

While the United States operated under the values of democracy and capitalism, where individuals are free to choose their own careers and lifestyles, the Soviet Union was run by

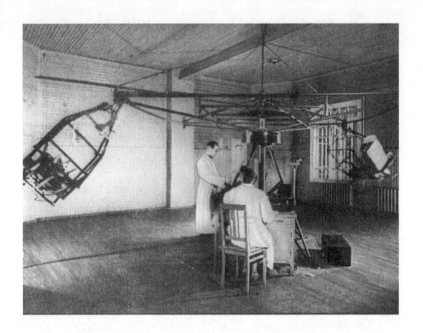

the Communist Party, which maintained stricter control over its people's resources and opportunities. One way the Soviet Union taught its Communist values to children was through the Young Pioneers, a popular club similar to the Boy Scouts and Girl Scouts of America. Members attended summer camps, performed service projects, learned pro-Communist songs and anthems, and played a war game called Zarnitsa, designed to train them to be future soldiers and nurses.

Though the Soviet Union prided itself on having more equal rights for women and the poor, the Communist Party dictated what could be taught in schools and reported on in newspapers, where citizens could travel, and often what work they could pursue. Anyone who disagreed with the government could be put into jail or a labor camp.

Many people feared that the political tensions between the United States and the Soviet Union would lead to war, so both sides began to develop better missiles and defense capabilities, and as a part of that, space technology. This began an era called the space race, where the two countries competed to be the first to send a person into orbit. The space race was about not only national security, but also ideology and culture. While the Soviet Union had many successes, such as sending Laika to space in 1957 and the first person to space in 1961, the United States succeeded in landing the first people on the moon in 1969.

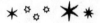

The Russians love dogs. This has been done not for the sake of cruelty but for the benefit of humanity.
—First Secretary Yuri Modin

HOW LAIKA CHANGED THE WORLD

When the world learned that the Soviets were launching a living creature into space, it became the most sensational news of the day. Newspapers from the United States, Australia, England, France, Germany, and many other countries ran articles speculating about the dog and her mission, since the Soviets kept almost all details secret at the time. Cafés and restaurants in the United States got new names, like the Orbit or the Cosmos. Long lines formed outside planetariums. In England, they called Laika "Muttnik" and "Pupnik"—plays on Sputnik II, the name of her rocket. Space-dog-themed stamps, coins, toys, and cigarette cases became wildly popular collectibles.

Many people around the world strongly objected to the use of animals as space test subjects, both by the US and the Soviet governments. One pro-animal activist, Mary Riddell, wrote to the Soviet embassy, "Your Government once again proved its inhumanity." And a British group, the National Canine Defense League, proposed holding a minute of silence every day until Laika returned home. Perhaps many Soviet citizens and scientists felt the same way, though in general Soviets were more comfortable with the idea of sacrifice in the pursuit of scientific knowledge and saw Laika's mission as a cause to be celebrated, not mourned. The popularity of the space dog program did have the positive result that throughout Soviet schools, students were taught how to be kind to street dogs, just like in Nina's class.

While we may still argue whether Laika's mission was ethical, the scientific breakthroughs that came from the Sputnik II program and the missions that followed it resulted in our modern technological age. Besides advancing space travel, discoveries from the space race era led to the development of smartphones, high-definition television, modern cameras, satellite communications, GPS software, radiology, robotics, artificial limbs, and even the laptop I wrote this book on. The world would look very different today if Laika had never taken off in her rocket.

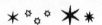

A LASTING MEMORY

Nina is fictional, but one of the head scientists did bring Laika home several nights before her launch so she could play with his children. He says of Laika, "I wanted to do something nice for her: she had so little time left to live." In 2008, the Russians erected a memorial dedicated to Laika outside a military facility, where thousands of visitors a year from around the world come to honor her life.

RECOMMENDED READING

If you want to read more about Laika and the other space dogs, these are some excellent places to start:

Abadzis, Nick. *Laika.* New York: First Second, 2007.

Burgess, Colin, and Chris Dubbs. *Animals in Space: From Research Rockets to the Space Shuttle.* New York: Springer, 2007.

Caswell, Kurt. *Laika's Window: The Legacy of a Soviet Space Dog.* San Antonio, TX: Trinity University Press, 2018.

D'Antonio, Michael. *A Ball, a Dog, and a Monkey: 1957—The Space Race Begins.* New York: Simon & Schuster, 2008.

Janus, Alan. *Animals Aloft: Photographs from the Smithsonian National Air and Space Museum.* Charlestown, MA: Bunker Hill Publishing, 2005.

Turkina, Olesya. *Soviet Space Dogs.* Translated by Inna Cannon and Lisa Wasserman. London: Fuel Design and Publishing, 2014.

ACKNOWLEDGMENTS

I am eternally grateful for the hardworking individuals who helped bring this book to my readers. The team at FSG, including Elizabeth Lee, Cassie Gonzales, Aurora Parlagreco, Valerie Shea, Hayley Jozwiak, and Allyson Floridia, treated Laika's story with all the grace and respect her true history deserves. My editor, Grace Kendall, knew just when to push, when to hold back, and challenged me to find the heart of the story. A special thanks to Josh Adams, who believed in this book from the beginning. It meant everything to me.

There were many readers who slogged through messy first drafts: Megan Miranda, Carrie Ryan, Beth Revis and the Bat Cave writers, and especially Rebecca Petruck, whose insights are on every page. If she hadn't reached out to offer encouragement at a time when I almost gave up, this book wouldn't exist.

Marcia Smith, editor of the *Space Policy* journal and a Fellow of the American Institute of Aeronautics and Astronautics, was kind enough to lend me her expertise, as did Dr. Cathleen Lewis of the Smithsonian Institution for my depiction of Soviet life and culture.

Lastly, to my husband and children, who gave me ample time and support to write this story, and to Bascom, my own scruffy mutt, who came into our lives unexpectedly and saved my son's life during a medical crisis. You showed me that heroes don't have to be human. You are in my heart forever, sweet pup.